The First Cut

A Jane Renwick Thriller #1

Val Penny

www.darkstroke.com

Discover us online:
www.darkstroke.com

Join us on instagram:
www.instagram.com/darkstrokebooks/

Include **#darkstroke** in a photo of yourself
holding this book on Instagram and
something nice will happen.

To my cousin Jean, with love

About the Author

This is the first in the new series of novels, The Jane Renwick Thrillers. Val Penny's other crime novels, Hunter's Chase Hunter's Revenge, Hunter's Force Hunter's Blood and Hunter's Secret form the bestselling series The Edinburgh Crime Mysteries. They are set in Edinburgh, Scotland, published by darkstroke Her first non-fiction book Let's Get Published is also available now and she has most recently contributed her short story, Cats and Dogs to a charity anthology, Dark Scotland.

Val is an American author living in SW Scotland with her husband and their cat.

Acknowledgements

Writing is often portrayed as a lonely occupation but while the story created here is the product of one mind, the process as a whole is far from solitary.

First, I must thank my beta readers and those who took time to read an early draft, critique and endorse The First Cut. Particular mentions must go to Michelle Cook, Austrian Spencer, Kate Braithwaite and Helen Matthews for their encouragement and help in offering suggestions and improvements. I must also thank Stewart Penny who always generously advises on physical training exercises and keeps my characters far fitter than I am.

I am also grateful to my editor, Laurence Patterson, one of the most patient people I have ever met, and to all at darkstroke books, including Steph Paterson for her help with creating the blurb for The First Cut. Without them, this book would not exist. I am also grateful to those who gave me medical and technical advice. Of course, any mistakes are mine.

My long-suffering and supportive husband, Dave deserves a special mention for his unconditional support as do our beloved girls, Lizzie, Vicky and Becca just because they are. And to each and every one of my readers, thank you. I am thrilled you enjoy my novels.

To Anne

The First Cut
A Jane Renwick Thriller #1

with love and thanks
for your support,

Val xx

Prologue

Evening. Friday, 21st September 1990

"I hope that woman's wrong and there aren't any kids in this flat. It smells disgusting. Do you want a sniff?" The social worker, Joan McCallum, slammed the letter box and turned to the younger policeman who stood behind her.

"Why on earth would I want to do that? I can smell it from here. It's honking."

"Officer, do you agree it's bloody stinking in there?" Joan asked.

He nodded. "No doubt about it."

"Then we need to get in and see if there are any kids. I know it's a nosy neighbour complaint, but we can't risk it. We would be lambasted for not acting and leaving children in there." She looked at the senior police officer behind her and wrinkled her nose. She took a deep breath and opened the letter box again. "Can you open the door, sir?" She turned back to the police officers. "It's John Smith, isn't it?"

"That's right."

"Mr. Smith, we've had a complaint that there may be children inside who are suffering neglect," she shouted. Someone moved inside, but there was no reply. Further down the hallway a door opened, and a neighbour poked their head out. Joan looked at her. "Please close your door, madam," she said. Then woman closed the door behind her and continued to stare. Joan sighed, then turned to the policemen again. "You better force the door."

"Move aside. We'll break the door down if they won't open it," the senior policeman shouted.

"Did you hear that? The police will break in if you won't

3

open up," she called again. "Come on. Just open the door and then we'll have a quick look and go away…" under her breath she said, "…with or without the children, as needs be."

Joan peered through the letter box again and saw a tall, skinny man stagger towards the door. He leant on the wall to turn the key in the lock, then weaved his way back along the corridor without opening the door. She turned the handle. The smell of urine, stale beer, tobacco, weed, and rotten vegetables floated towards her on a sea of dirt and grease.

She followed him along the corridor and into the dirty living room. A heavily pregnant woman lay on the filthy sofa. She was gouching on heroin and held a can of special brew. The man who had unlocked the door sat on the floor in front of her, rubbed her extended belly, and smoked a joint.

"Are there any children here?" Joan asked.

The man laughed and rubbed faster, shouting. "Well, there's one in here!" He giggled hysterically as if he'd made a fine joke.

"Yes, I'd guess we'll need to take that one as soon as it's born, but are there any others?"

"Nah, not here, love. Nay kiddies in here." He laughed again and crossed his fingers. The pregnant woman grinned and revealed black spaces where teeth should have been.

"Aye, nane here, hen," the woman cackled.

"I'll take a look around, shall I?"

Neither appeared to have heard what she'd said, or they didn't care, so Joan proceeded up the hallway and pushed open the doors to the other rooms one by one. There was clearly nobody in the bathroom or kitchen. Both were covered in detritus and the floors stuck to her shoes.

She knocked the first bedroom door open with the elbow of her coat. A filthy, unmade double bed dominated the small room. Joan bent down to look underneath it and found herself staring at three pairs of eyes set in grubby little faces. The children could not stay here, of that, she was sure. She became aware of the man who swayed unsteadily behind her.

"You're no' takin' they weans," he said.

"I think you'll find we are. Officer, please restrain Mr

4

Smith." She spoke with authority and moved past both the policeman and the occupier. Then Joan crouched down on her haunches. Her demeanour and tone changed completely. "Come on, out you come," she said gently. She ignored the man and enticed the children with an offer of small bars of chocolate. "I think you could each do with one of these."

"Each?" the little girl in the middle asked.

"Of course, each. Nobody likes to share chocolate. You come out and I'll get some of your clothes packed into a bag while you eat it."

"No, Janey. You stay put. I'll get you some chocolate." The man whined.

"He won't," the oldest child said as he wriggled towards Joan. "Let's go with her. Come on Janey, Craig. I'm starving." The younger two followed his lead and moved forward. The boy was right when he said he was starving. The children's limbs were like sticks. Bruises were clearly visible, and she didn't think any of them had seen a bath for long enough. The three stood in front of her with their hands out. She gave each the small bar they had been promised and noticed that the older boy unwrapped the treat for his younger sister and brother before he gobbled down his own chocolate.

"You don't have any more, do you Mrs?" he asked.

"No but we'll get you some soup and sandwiches when I get you to the home."

"You're no' takin' my kiddies, hen. I'll no' let you."

"Officers," she called.

The second policemen also entered the house and stood between the man and his children.

"You cannae let her take them away," the father screamed.

She ignored him and the policemen did not answer. From the expressions on their faces, she deduced they did not want to breathe in any more of the rancid air than they had to.

"Where will we find your clean clothes?" she asked the children, more in hope than expectation.

"You'll be lucky," said the girl. "If there are any they'll be here" She led the way into the room next door. There was a set of bunk beds and a cot. Under the window, there was also a small chest of three drawers. The girl pulled out a few things from each one. "We all have our own drawer, and that's about all that's clean," she said.

"No problem. We can get you other stuff at the home," Joan replied. The few articles they had were bundled into her bag, "Do you have any favourite toys or books you want to take?"

Each child picked up a toy from the floor and turned to her for approval.

"That's fine. Whatever you want."

The littlest one climbed into a bottom bunk and grabbed a dirty toy giraffe.

"Any more for anymore?" she asked in an overly jolly voice. "No, then we'll be off. Get your coats."

The oldest child reached for the soiled jackets on the back of the bedroom door and helped his siblings before he put on his own fleece.

"Don't take my kids. Get up woman, they're taking our kids. Stop them!" he shouted at the woman who lay comatose on the couch.

"And I'll be back for that one when they arrive," Joan said under her breath, and she led the three children down the stairs to her waiting car. The older boy held her hand while the policemen carried the girl and her younger brother. As they settled the children into the back seat of her car, she spoke to them almost apologetically.

"At this time of night," Joan said to the officers. "I couldn't get all three with the one family. The boys will stay together in Fairmilehead, but I've had to place the girl separately in Trinity. It's the best I could do. Will you go back to arrest the parents?"

"For drug abuse, if nothing else." They nodded and whispered with her before she got into the car and drove away.

That was the last time Jane saw any members of her family.

Chapter One

Evening. 15th May 2014

What the hell? Who is that guy? He wasn't meant to be here! Where was the woman? Fuck. He realised he'd been seen. He acted casual.

"Where's Joy?"

"Joy who?"

The guy must be foreign; he's got a funny accent.

"Joy Tuesday, my aunt. She said she'd be here, I need to find her to drive her home." Lies came easily to him, they always had. *'Blame whoever's not in the room, that'll keep the group together,' they'd said. Ridiculous, look how well that had worked.*

"Don't know that name, but there's nobody else here right now. I'm working. Please just go away."

He felt the blow of dismissal, like everybody had always dismissed him. How dare they? How dare he? This foreigner didn't even belong here. None of them did. None of them deserved the time of day, never mind the air they breathed. He would soon stop all that.

He smiled and took a few steps into the room.

"What you busy with? It's late to be working." He walked around the desk, took out his blade, and punched it into his victim's carotid artery with practised precision. He dragged the blade across the neck to slice the artery, a quick second slice to make sure, but the first cut was the deepest. He made no errors, no mistakes. There was no hesitation. His victim stared at him, clutching his throat as the life blood ran out of him. All over the desk, all over the laptop computer, all over the important work that had required his dismissal. The blood sprayed over the desk, spattered the bookcase and into his mouth. That tinny, metallic taste he had come to enjoy. He would need to wipe his face before he left the room. It was a lucky break that he had a packet of tissues.

He smiled as his victim held his neck, the struggle, the gurgle, the death rattle of the man who tried to hold the life sustaining liquid in his body. They all did that. Again, ridiculous. It would never work. Not for long. It splashed through his fingers and onto the floor. That carpet hadn't been up to much before, and it wasn't worth shit now.

The man flopped over the desk. He wondered if that action had broken the laptop. Not that he really cared, the computer would come with him anyway. He grimaced. Having to rummage through the bloody pockets to get the phone was nasty, but he didn't want to leave anything behind. Good! Got it first time. A decent one. It would get a bob or two.

He chuckled as he thought how confusing this would be, because this one didn't fit with the profiles of the other victims at all. It wasn't possible, this one had nothing to do with anything. Maybe it was a good thing he had missed her. Good name he came up with too, Joy Tuesday. Pity nobody would ever know or be able to share it. Poor Policeman Plod. This one would make no sense, yet they would have to make it fit.

He left as quietly as he had come, laptop under one arm, phone in his pocket, bloody blade in his belt. Then he saw her, the right fucking woman, whatever her name was, he couldn't remember now because of the excitement. The green flash at the front of her hair was quite endearing. This evening, she had had a lucky escape, but he would be back.

Chapter Two

Several members of the murder investigation team were moving around the edges of the incident room, just going about their business, working different cases while others, including the civilian staff, lingered around to listen to the briefing the Superintendent was about to give. Those individuals were still not inured to the perverse and peculiar excitement crackling around the room, thankfully, but small gatherings like this one were few and far between.

The killer they had gathered to talk about was unusual too.

His personal connection to the team added a frisson that none of them had encountered before. Superintendent Graham Miller and Detective Chief Inspector Allan Mackay had sent Detective Sergeant Jane Renwick home, and now Miller stood, ready to address the dozen or so detectives assembled around the desks closest to him. They were the core members of his team. For many, this would be the biggest case they had ever worked. Miller believed he could not only taste the adrenalin but also smell it, as the detectives lived in fear of dropping the ball and letting him down, or, more specifically, Renwick.

Miller heard the pencils rapping on the edges of desks. He cleared his throat and wiped his hands against his stubble.

"This operation is now focused on one person who we strongly suspect has killed three times in the past five months. You have details of all those crimes in the notes in front of you." Miller watched as pages were turned. He waited for the rustle of paper to die down and then turned to the white board behind him. "Moving forward, we must focus all our attention on his most recent victim, Dr Zelay Scheptytsky, aged thirty-eight who was murdered four days ago in his office at the University of Edinburgh. His carotid artery was slashed."

Although there was a photo of Zelay Sheptytsky contained in every set of briefing notes, Miller was aware that most of the detectives had now looked up from their pages. They were staring past him to the glossy eight by ten on the white board, and he turned to look at the picture himself. The photograph had been taken by Zelay's colleague, Dr Gillian Pearson, at a party given by her boyfriend, Tim Myerscough, a Detective Constable based in Edinburgh about a year previously.

"Most investigations need a bit of luck," Miller said. He continued to stare at the photograph and then his gaze drifted back to his team. "They all need a break. We've been lucky, and it seems that this break may be the one we need. We have traced new leads and new evidence. For the first time, our culprit left a bloody handprint on the desk, presumably when he disconnected the laptop."

Miller turned around and noticed all eyes of the team were on him. "Zelay Sheptytsky was not lucky, and neither was his family, nor those who cared about him, including his seventy-year-old mother, his friends and his students." Miller nodded to DC Angus McKenzie, one of the newer members of the team who was scribbling in his notebook.

"Yes, son. Write it all down. Read it to yourself first thing every morning and last thing each night. Tattoo it on your arse if it helps you remember, because those are the people we work for and, if we do our jobs properly, the moment will come when the man we are after will run clean out of his measure of luck, once and for all."

He watched the new member of Police Scotland's MIT blush and chew the end of his pencil like a little boy. Miller saw McKenzie's embarrassment. It had been wrong to pick on the lad. He paused and let what he had said sink in for a few more seconds, while he thought about his next actions. He walked over to the young DC and tapped him on the shoulder.

"Don't worry, we'll get him. We just need to do that before he kills anybody else," he said. He moved back to lean against a desk and made room for DCI Allan Mackay to take over.

"Right." Mackay stood up. "We are working on the assumption that our killer made contact with Zelay Sheptytsky before the day he was killed. We need to find out how."

"And do we *know* the murderer is related to Jane?" Angus asked.

"Biologically, yes. The DNA he left at the last two crime scenes has established that."

"So does she know who he is and what he looks like? That would be a huge help."

"No, and no." Mackay spoke shortly. The young DC blushed again; his mouth stretched into a thin line. He didn't ask any more questions.

Had Jane not been sent home, Miller would have been happy to hand the briefing over to her and let her answer those private questions as far as she thought were relevant at this stage. However, in the circumstances, he was happy to leave the nuts and bolts to DCI Allan Mackay. He had not been at MIT long, but was an experienced officer with whom all the team were familiar. In truth, at this point, Jane's present absence had advantages. She was a capable officer, but she was only a DS, and she was too personally involved to work this crime.

Right now, it was more fitting that Mackay crack the whip and continue to address the team than that Miller pull rank. He listened to Mackay. "Our suspect appears to have taken Zelay's phone and laptop. This was also true of his earlier victims. We think he does that because it would make it absolutely clear how he made contact if we found them. He's not stealing these things on the spur of the moment, and we need to find out what he is trying to cover up."

"Perhaps emails and texts?" DC Amar Patel asked.

"That's what we're thinking," Mackay said. "We need to talk to Zelay's mobile provider and see what we can access." He nodded at the predictable groans from those who had trodden that tedious path before. They were all well-aware of the endless paperwork and the time-consuming and extensive set of protocols. "I know, it's a nightmare, and by the time we get anything out of them we'll probably all be collecting our pensions, but let's get on with it and get the process started."

"What about social media?" Amar asked.

"Good idea. That too," Mackay replied. "Zelay's colleague, Dr Gillian Pearson, told the local team that Zelay had a Facebook account and was active on Twitter and Instagram. We must assume they are all real possibilities. We need to get on to that.

"All of the victims were single, so should we think about dating apps like Tinder or dating websites?" Amar said as he looked at Mackay with a grin on his face.

"And maybe Grindr," a voice from the back of the group quipped.

"Absolutely. But it's not going to be easy without access to the search history for the victim."

There was more nodding and scribbling from the team followed by an outbreak of chatter. Mackay raised his voice above it.

"While some of you are working on all of that, we need to trace Zelay's movements throughout the day he was killed. We're presuming that he had been out at some point because he had no classes at the university except for a small seminar between four and five in the afternoon and he had to eat. He may have met his killer before or after lunch time. We need to know where he went. Zelay was seen having lunch in the university dining hall. His body was found in his own office by the cleaners early this morning. Obviously we need to be looking at CCTV. The team in Edinburgh have made a start on that, so make sure to liaise with them.

"There was alcohol in Zelay's blood," Miller said. "The chances are that if and when he went out, he didn't drive, but check the ANPR just in case and then talk to all the taxi and private hire car companies in the city."

Mackay looked up from his notes. "The post-mortem identified semi-digested pasta in his stomach, so he probably ate dinner out that evening. Check with the restaurants that serve pasta near the university. See if they recognise his photo. You'll need to work with the local uniforms to get this done quickly because we need to find out where he went and if he was meeting anybody."

"Gillian, his colleague, may know if there were any

restaurants nearby that he used more than others," Angus suggested.

"True. You know her, don't you, Angus?"

"Yes, sir."

"Phone her and ask about that. Be discreet. I understand she is very fragile."

Miller drew the meeting to a close. "DCI Mackay, can you divide all those duties amongst the team?"

Mackay grunted in thanks or acknowledgement; Miller wasn't sure which. He walked back to his office listening to Allan Mackay.

Chapter Three

Jane pulled the helmet onto her well-coiffed hair. She knew it would ruin the style, but she had rarely cared less. The power of the Harley Davidson throbbed beneath her, and the wheels tore along the motorway leading home to Edinburgh. She wove between the cars and vans that moved within the speed-limit.

Tears streamed down her cheeks as the warm air flew past her face. All these years she had longed for a family she could love, brothers she might cherish again, but she had found out it was just a dream, and her nightmare would continue. She was even prevented from doing the job she loved until the beast that was related to her was caught.

Jane was only permitted to attend court in a professional capacity in the few outstanding, unrelated cases where she was a witness. Could life get any worse? She opened the throttle and put her head down. Riding faster usually improved her mood, but not today.

Jane sped back to Fettes Station in Edinburgh. It seemed to be the logical place to go. She took off her helmet, thumped the door open, strode past DS Charlie Middleton, and ran upstairs to DI Hunter Wilson's office.

Jane forgot to knock.

Her partner, DC Rachael Anderson, was sitting in Hunter's room, weeping. Jane noticed Hunter frown and hand Rachael a box of tissues from the top drawer of the desk.

They both looked up and stared at Jane.

"Oh, darling. I'm so sorry," Rachael said. She stood up, stepped towards Jane, and hugged her tightly. "How on earth did you get here so quickly?"

"Don't answer that," Hunter said. "You know you cannot be

here and must take no part in this investigation either with your MIT colleagues or with us at local level. Superintendent Miller will have told you that."

"He did. I only have a few witness appearances that I must attend in court on cases that have nothing to do with this nightmare. Boss, the thing is, I don't know this man. It's not as if we're really family. I haven't clapped eyes on him since I was five years old. Let me help. Please, just let me help."

"You know I can't do that, even if I wanted to. I know you have leave from MIT, Jane, so why doesn't Rachael take some well-earned time off too? You are definitely due some." Hunter's gaze flicked over to Rachael. "It would allow you both to unwind, relax, and enjoy each other's company. What do you think?"

Jane smiled at Rachael. She had never learned to cry neatly. Snot and mascara clotted on her cheeks. Jane reached for a couple of Hunter's tissues and licked them before wiping Rachael's face.

"That's a good idea, boss. I think I better stop into the loo and wash my face before I go anywhere."

"It's settled then. Don't worry about the paperwork, I'll sort it. Look after each other."

"Can I pop in to see the team while Rache gets cleaned up?"

"I'm sorry, Jane. You know that I can't allow that," he said. "I'll have to escort you out of the station to your bike," Hunter said. He stood up and turned to Rachael. "Will you drive yourself home, or do you want to travel with Jane? I can get a PC assigned to take your car back for you."

"No thanks, boss. Riding with Jane is far too nerve-wracking for me. I like four wheels, within the speed limit, thank you very much." Rachael smiled a weak, watery smile. "Thanks for the time, boss. Janey, I'll just go and get cleaned up and see you back home." She kissed Jane gently on the cheek before she left the room.

Jane swung her gaze slowly around to Hunter, one eyebrow arched "How did they find out he was related to me?"

"After the cases at the end of last year, our elimination

DNA databases were recategorised to be routinely included in our investigations. DC Nadia Chan and DS Colin Reid wrote a report and suggested how we could check all the databases more efficiently going forward."

"And there I was."

"And there you were, full sibling to our suspect."

"We know he's my brother, just not his identity, where he lives or what he looks like. That's insane. And because of that freak of nature, I am off the case, and now Rachael is too. It's crazy."

"You remember having two brothers, don't you, Jane?"

"Yes, one older, one younger, but we got separated in the foster care system. And of course, I was only wee, but I remember my mother saying we were getting a baby for Christmas. None of us were that chuffed because there was little enough to eat as it was. It does mean there may be another child, even younger. I suppose there could be several. I never saw my parents after I was removed by the social worker.

"Okay, boss. I'll go home now. I'll phone to enter my court appearances into the diary. Thank you for giving Rachael the time off. We both really appreciate it."

Hunter opened his office door and held it open for her, He patted Jane on the arm, and she put her motorcycle helmet back on. "It'll sort itself out. You'll see," he said as they walked together through the station and to the carpark. Jane climbed onto her bike, put it in gear, and roared off towards the home she shared with Rachael in the popular suburb of Bruntsfield.

***

Rachael reached the flat half an hour after Jane. She had stopped off for a bottle of crisp white wine, a selection of cheeses, some grapes, olives, and a box of crackers. She knew they had Parma ham and hummus in the refrigerator. Rachael also knew neither of them would want to cook that evening, so a tasty selection for a mezze was her way of making sure they didn't just eat crisps and chocolate all evening.

Jane peered into the shopping bag and took out the wine.

"I'll put this into the fridge, but let's leave the cheese out so we get the full flavours. What did you get?"

"I saw a nice piece of blue stilton, a double Gloucester with beer and chives, and an extremely ripe brie. I thought that would be enough for the two of us."

"It all sounds delicious. Thank you for thinking of this because I really don't want to cook."

"Neither of us do. Shall we get that bottle of Prosecco out of the fridge and run a warm bubble bath? It's early, so we can eat after relaxing properly. I can see the tension in your shoulders, Janey, and it's not good for you."

"Now that, my dear Rachael, is the best idea anybody has had today. I'll get the Prosecco and you run the bath. I'll be with you in two minutes."

"Last one through gets the tap end." Rachael giggled. They had installed a large, new bath with central taps when they moved into the flat. Neither of them ever got the tap end, but it was a running joke between them.

Jane picked the cold bottle from the fridge and reached for two plastic champagne flutes from the kitchen cupboard. At least if they dropped them, they wouldn't break.

She glanced out of the kitchen window and into the communal back green of their apartment block. There was a man standing in the garden looking up at her. She frowned. She didn't recognise him, but he looked familiar. She stared towards him and then suddenly, as if he had just noticed her, he pulled up the hood of his jacket and jumped over the back wall into the garden beyond.

She watched him race across the gardens, one after another until he reached the corner. She lost sight of him when he turned towards the shops.

"Janey, where are you? I'm getting lonely and the bath water is getting cold. Come on girl. If I'd wanted to bathe on my own, I'd have locked the door."

Jane wandered through to the bathroom and sat on the lid of the toilet. She told Rachael what she had seen.

"What if it's my brother looking for me?"

"Don't be daft! It's probably just a chancer trying to see if any of the flats look empty. If he finds a likely contender, he'd try his hand at the door and see what's there for the taking. Now." Rachael slid up the bath revealing her full breasts and brushed her hands down her body. "Does anybody want to share this bath with me?"

Jane handed her a glass of the bubbly and pretended to let her hand slip. The cold, wet wine ran across Rachael's nipples, and they reacted immediately, becoming tight and hard. Jane knelt beside her and cupped her left breast in her hand, sucking the nipple excitedly and pulled off her clothes before she scrabbled into the warm water.

The water was cool, and the wine warm before they got out of the bath and dried themselves off.

"Let's not get dressed. We'll just cuddle up in our dressing gowns and nibble our way through the cheese, shall we?" Jane suggested.

"Good idea. And then will you tell me what exactly is going on? You've never really said much about your family or your life before we met."

"I haven't, have I? Well, now is probably as good a time as any for you to know."

Chapter Four

DC Amar Patel had been paired with the newbie to the team, DC Angus McKenzie. He was not much enamoured with his ginger haired partner, or his highland accent, but decided to make the best of a bad job. He noticed Angus frowning over the list of victims and their known social media profiles. Angus looked up at Amar and spoke quietly and deliberately.

"I'm going to get a coffee. You want anything?"

"Tea, milk and one. Remember that."

Angus ignored the barbed comment. When he came back with the drinks, he began to speak in his highland accent again. "The first two victims were a lot older than the professor."

"True, so what?" Amar asked. He didn't acknowledge the tea.

"Well, aren't they less likely to have a social media presence?"

"Could be, but we know Dolores Cline was a designer and Beatrice Dalgleish was a poet. They are likely to have had a presence on social media for their careers, if for no other reason. Don't you think?" Amar watched Angus nod slowly. The man was going to drive him mad. Couldn't he just speed up a bit? Or maybe he should try to wind Angus up to make him go faster.

"Two of the victims are older women. The professor doesn't fit that profile at all. That bothers me," Angus said.

"No, but he is a professional and foreign born."

"Dalgleish doesn't sound very foreign to me. It's a good Scottish name."

"But Dubois isn't."

"What?" Angus looked puzzled.

"She married a Scot. Her own name was Dubois, remember. She was born in Paris."

"Did I know that?"

"If you read the briefing notes, you did." Amar watched with satisfaction as the tall highlander blushed red to the roots of his hair. He sat down at the nearest computer and glowered at the screen. "You make a list of all the social media platforms. We might get email addresses for Dolores or Beatrice from one of those."

"I just had a thought."

"First time for everything, I suppose."

"You are an arse, you know that?"

"Is that your thought? If so, you're not the first person to think it," Amar sneered.

"We may not have the victims' phones or computers because they're with forensics, but Zelay worked at the university."

"Brilliant. The professor worked at the university."

"Just shut it, Patel. I've had enough of you."

"That makes two of us. Anyway, what are you getting at?"

"My guess is that the university has a mainframe, LAN or WAN, where the professor's work and entries would be stored out with his own hard drive."

"LAN, WAN. What are you on about?"

"Don't you know? LAN stands for Local Area Network and it's when computers that are physically close together are connected either wirelessly or with cables."

"Really? And what about a WAN?"

"That acronym stands for Wide Area Network. It's the same idea but because the computers are further apart telephone cables or even satellites are likely to be used to connect them and send information between them."

"Even Zelay's laptop?"

"If it was plugged on and attached to the network, yes."

"You know, if the university has that, then we could find his emails really quickly. It would be a real feather in our caps. You contact the university and talk to the person who would know. Good luck finding them." Amar smiled and was unnerved when Angus smiled back cheerfully.

He watched Angus pull his mobile out of his jacket pocket and dial. The call was answered quickly.

"Hello, Gillian. Yes, it's Angus… Yes, it's too awful. Such a respected man. How are you? …It must have been a terrible shock…. Have you heard from Zelay's family?... Of course. Dreadful…. They are lucky that you speak such good Ukrainian so you could explain properly what had happened and what was going on…. No, it must have been really difficult for you."

Amar scowled at Angus. "Get on with it," he whispered.

"There is something you might be able to assist me with," Angus said. "It might help to find the killer… Yes, really… What it is, Gillian? Are the computers in your department linked to some kind of mainframe through an LAN or WAN?" There was a slight pause and then Angus's face broke into a wide smile, and he gave Amar a thumbs up. "Would that even apply to Zelay's laptop?... Great that's what I thought. Who do I need to speak to?... Will he be able to give me transcripts?... Do you think he'll insist on a warrant? Some of the stuff we need is recent." Amar saw Angus nod solemnly. "I'll speak to DCI Mackay and get that put into motion. Thanks Gillian, and if you see Jane, tell her we're working our fingers to the bone to solve this for her. I think I'm playing squash with Tim on Friday? Okay. Take care of yourself. Keep in touch. Aye, thanks a lot."

Amar looked at Angus.

"Sorted," Angus said, without enlightening Amar further. "Want to come with me and tell Mackay what we've got?"

"I don't know what we've got."

"Well, you could stay and check out all the social media platforms," Angus said. He turned on his heels and marched towards the DCI's office. Amar followed him. He didn't want to be left out. Angus knocked gently on the door and walked in.

"McKenzie, Patel. What can I do for you?" Amar noticed that Mackay was looking at him and felt uncomfortable.

"You explain it, Angus," he said.

"I was thinking, sir, that Zelay Scheplesky's computer

21

might be linked into a university mainframe of some sort, perhaps on a LAN or WAN and we might be able to get copies of his entries from that."

"What a good idea. How did you get on wading your way through the hundreds of members of staff at The University of Edinburgh?"

"Well, I took a short-cut, sir and called Dr Gillian Pearson, his colleague."

"Of course. Fine woman. And you know her personally, don't you?"

"Yes, sir. I'm also friendly with her boyfriend."

"I remember. How is she bearing up through all of this? It must have been a real shock for the department. And especially for Dr Pearson because she worked closely with Dr Scheptytsky."

"She's really upset but she was able to help us. Even though Zelay was working on his laptop, if it was plugged into the university system, we can get copies of the contents on his hard drive. Gillian gave me the name and contact details for the chap, but she's sure he'll want a warrant."

"I'm not at all surprised. Let's get that arranged, and then I think you fellows may need to make a trip to Edinburgh. What do you have to add to the party, Amar?"

Chapter Five

Rachael set out their casual meal on the coffee table in front of the sofa. She brought through cutlery, pretty plates, and crystal glasses, and unscrewed the wine. She poured them each a glass of the crisp Pinot Grigio, and cuddled up beside Jane.

"Now, where do you want to start, Janey?"

"With the brie and this glass of wine."

Rachael sat on the sofa beside Jane and reached for the plates. She offered the crackers to Jane and watched her choose from the tasty selection before Jane cut the largest slice of brie imaginable. Rachael noticed that she ate the food without making eye contact with her. She watched as Jane pulled a small bunch of grapes from the stalk and ate them one by one. Rachael sighed.

"I'm not in any rush, Janey. If you want to take your time, I have no problem with that." Rachael picked a salty cracker, broke it into pieces and dipped it into the hummus.

"I never knew what it felt like to be loved before I met you," Jane whispered.

"I know I was not your first girlfriend, so that's not quite true."

"Oh, but it is. You see, the first two or three, well that was just lust when I was able to get out on my own. Spread my wings. Then I found myself without a roof over my head, so when Cherie made her move, she offered me the security of a home. Then I discovered what her day job was, or at least night job, so I left one evening when she was out and got a room in a flat with some students. One of them got me a job in the bar he worked in and thought I would be more grateful than I wanted to be. There I was again, out on the streets and no job, but at least I could pull a decent pint."

Rachael smiled and held Jane's hand. "Yuck, your fingers are covered in sticky brie."

"You can talk, you've got garlicy hummus all over yours."

They both laughed. The silence hung in the air as Rachael sat quietly and watched Jane gather her thoughts. Then she listened, while Jane spoke about her brothers for the first time. Donny and Craig, the protector and the protected. What had happened to them? How had their lives turned out? Were they even alive? Was the baby she had never met a boy or a girl? Even if she had a sister, their relationship could never be like Rachael's with her sister Sarah.

Rachael sat eating cheese and ham and watched Jane sipping wine. She waited for Jane to start speaking again.

"I managed to get a job in The Beehive pub in the Grassmarket. It could be a bit wild, especially at the weekends, but the manager had a spare bedroom in his flat above the pub. He offered me a room if I would go in early and wash any dirty glasses left from the night before and set up for opening."

"That sounds okay, as long as he was decent with you."

"He was, but his boyfriend was a real pig. I ended up as house maid to them as well as barmaid in the pub."

"Hmm. Typical."

"It was also pretty full-on seven days a week, but the pay was good, and he paid me properly, through the books."

"What went wrong?"

"Nothing. I saved and saved and decided to set myself goals. The first one was to rent a place on my own. I got a wee one-bedroom flat up in Gorgie through a private housing association. It only had a kitchen/living room, bedroom and bathroom, but it was all I needed, and it was all mine."

"No more girlfriends to love you?"

"No. I lived very quietly. I doubt most of my neighbours knew I was even there. Far from being loved, I was invisible. I sometimes wondered, if I died in the night, how long it would take anybody to notice."

"Oh, Janey, sweetheart. I hate to think of you feeling like that." Rachael moved closer and hugged her tight. "You would be noticed, now, dreadfully missed, and you would always be remembered as the fabulous, beautiful clever woman you are, were."

"Don't lay it on too thick, Rache. I'm just saying how I felt then."

"I know. Want more wine?"

"Is the Pope a Catholic?" Jane held her glass out to Rachael and watched the pale liquid splash up the sides of the bowl. "Anyway, I left The Beehive to work in a pub nearby my flat to minimise travel costs and then set my sights on my next goal."

"Which was?"

"To save more money and study to get into the police. I wanted to be as different from the family I was born into as possible and that was how I thought I could do it."

"If what the boss told me this afternoon is right, you have accomplished that."

Rachael looked into Jane's grey eyes and saw the tears streaming down her cheeks. She held her close and waited for them to subside. She rocked Jane in a rhythmic pattern and after what felt like an age, the crying stopped. Jane started to hiccup. Rachael lifted her chin and their eyes met. Jane hiccupped again and they both laughed.

"Go on, wash your face and then let's finish eating. I think that's enough reminiscing for one evening, Janey."

When Jane came back into the room, Rachael watched her curl up on the couch and choose a selection of things to eat. "Shall we watch *Gogglebox* or *Benidorm*?" Rachael asked. She knew that either ridiculous programme would lighten the mood for Jane.

"My, my. Aren't we the culture vultures?"

Chapter Six

Angus did not normally value one-upmanship. However, he would have paid money to hear what Amar and DC Judy Marsh were saying about him as they ate their lunch in the canteen together. He guessed they were talking about him from their glances and body language, which made it quite clear he should sit elsewhere.

"Come sit here, Angus," Brian Harris called over from a table near the window. "I heard you're a man with connections."

"Not really. I just know Professor Sheptytsky's colleague, Dr Gillian Pearson. She was able to give me a name that cut my morning's work to a tenth of what it would have been otherwise."

"Yeh, that's what Amar said." Brian smiled at Angus. It was well known that the DCs fell into two camps, Amar's allies, and Brian's bunch. "How do you know her?"

Angus had learned an old saying from his grandmother. 'Never make anybody as wise as yourself.' He felt he had not been at MIT long enough to choose between the groups and certainly did not feel able to trust either Amar or Brian, so he answered Brian exactly as he knew Amar had heard. "I'm friendly with her boyfriend." Angus tucked into his macaroni cheese more heartily than it deserved, but it did mean he was able to avoid having to discuss the matter further.

After lunch, Angus and Amar re-convened at their desks. "It'll be at least tomorrow before we get that warrant," Amar said. "Why don't you take Twitter and Instagram? I'll take Facebook and LinkedIn, and we'll see what we can find for each of our victims. We should cross-reference them, I suppose."

Angus nodded and pulled up a chair at his desk. He was

methodical in his approach and chose to start with each victim in turn on Instagram. The designer, Dolores Cline, had a substantial presence there. She had over a hundred thousand followers and Angus noticed that many of them were amongst the great and the good of show business, reality stars, and some even from the aristocracy. Under no circumstances did he plan to write down that number of names, so, as it was a public account, he went to the list of followers and printed it off.

He sighed when he moved to her Twitter account. The woman had over forty thousand followers. Angus decided that this called for the strong stuff.

"I'm getting a coffee. You want anything?"

"A six-foot blond," Amar replied.

"I'll see if Brian's available."

Amar smiled. "Go on then, I'll take a tea. Milk and…"

"One. Yes, I remember. I'm not a complete numpty."

When Angus got back with the drinks, he put Amar's on his desk. "How are you getting on?"

"This first one has more Facebook friends than I ever imagined. It's a bloody nightmare. And of course, she has a professional profile as well as her personal one and a professional page. I wish I'd given you Facebook."

"You wouldn't have been any happier with Instagram. She's got over a hundred thousand followers there. How do you interact with that many people?"

"You don't. You just tantalise the luvvies with your spectacular genius and tease them with trivia about your life. 'I made scrambled eggs for breakfast, with butter, aren't I the naughty one?' Things like that."

Angus laughed and sat down with his coffee. He ran off a printout of the Twitter followers and moved on to Beatrice, the poet. He was overjoyed to find that she had not ventured into the visual world of Instagram and had only seventeen thousand followers on Twitter. He took his usual printout and moved on to Zelay. Hallelujah! Sixteen followers on Instagram and two thousand and four on Twitter. This was doable. Angus clapped his hands, swigged the rest of his coffee, grabbed Amar's cup, and went to get them more drinks.

Later in the afternoon, Angus and Amar sat with their heads together going through the lists of followers. Some were eminently more manageable than others.

"Look. Both the women follow this dating web-site."

"That's interesting. Let's check it out. *Alone in a Crowd* is one of the biggest dating sites in the country. If you were going to dabble, it's an obvious one to choose Amar. Look. Dolores follows these ones on Twitter too."

"Yes, and she's 'liked' all the Facebook pages." Amar pointed to the sheets.

"Zelay wasn't interested in any of them."

"I think they tend to have more women than men signing up."

"And how are you such an expert?" Angus teased.

"I'm not. It's just what I've heard." Amar reddened and looked away.

Angus drew his attention back to the screen. "But look, here. Zelay has expressed interest in this speed dating event. I wonder if he went along."

"I don't know. But I can't think he made such a bad impression that he'd get murdered for it. I think we're barking up the wrong tree," Amar said.

"We probably are. What else do they have in common?"

"Both the women went to the same hairdresser. That's a bit of a coincidence."

"Not really, Amar. If you know Edinburgh, it's one of the big salons in the city centre. Fashionable and high priced. Does men and women. Is there anything to show that Zelay went there?"

"No. But I can't see a university professor traipsing into the city centre to pay a fortune for a haircut. Can you?"

"You're right. From his profile photo he certainly doesn't look like a fashion victim. Back to the drawing board."

Chapter Seven

Jane and Rachael woke from their restless sleep. Jane got up quickly and changed into her running shorts.

"What are you doing?" Rachael said, sleepily.

"I'm off for a run. I think it might clear my head. Looking back last night meant I didn't get much sleep. Too many things rolling around my mind. Do you want to join me?"

"Not in the slightest. I'll see you when you get back, pet." She wriggled out of bed, kissed Jane sweetly on the lips and wandered through to the bathroom for a hot, reviving shower.

Jane jogged down the stairs to the street. At the door of the building she stopped, pulled her phone out of her pocket, and put in her earphones before looking right and left and then jogging across the street. She jogged to the end of Bruntsfield Avenue and down Bruntsfield Place, towards the green area of Bruntsfield Links where she would run on the grass, and across the wide area of parkland until she was not thinking about the past anymore.

Perhaps if Jane had not had her earphones in, perhaps if she had not been listening to Kei$ha's song, Past Lives, perhaps if she hadn't been so deep in her own thoughts, then she might have noticed the tall, tattooed man sitting on the bench watching her. But she did not see him and did not notice him, even when she paused briefly to catch her breath. She ran around the park until the sweat was dripping from the end of her nose and she could not think about anything except for the pain in her muscles. She was so tired. She thought for a moment about taking a bus home, until she remembered that she hadn't brought any money.

She jogged slowly along Leamington Walk and was surprised by the tall, tattooed man who had appeared, as if from nowhere, in front of her. He looked her up and down until she felt distinctly uncomfortable. She took her earphones out and challenged him with a stare.

"Do you do that for pain or for pleasure?" he asked.

"What does it matter to you? Wait a minute, didn't I see you in my back green yesterday? Are you following me? Or stalking me? Who are you anyway?"

She saw a hint of a smile flit across his face, then he turned on his heels and strode away. She started to run after him, but a cramp stopped her, and she was left gasping in pain, staring at his back.

She limped home and pulled on the handrail to climb the stairs to their apartment. She groaned as she turned the key in the lock, and greeted Rachael with a grimace.

"Not a good look, Janey. Do you know you were away for nearly three hours? No wonder you're knackered."

Jane fetched a clean bath sheet from the cupboard and, without saying anything in reply, went into the bathroom and stepped into the shower, letting the hot water pour over her body, soothing her aches and pains. When she felt better again, she dried and dressed and went into the kitchen.

"What's for breakfast? I'm so hungry I could eat a scabby dog."

"I'm so sorry. The scabby dog has been so popular this morning that I am clean out of that. May I suggest the muesli or a croissant?"

"Do you think the budget would stretch to both? I'm ravenous."

"I'm not surprised. You've been out so long that if you'd been away any longer, I'd have called the cops." Rachael smiled.

"That might not have been a bad idea," Jane said. She told Rachael about the tattooed man while tucking into her muesli.

***

Jane changed into a dark navy suit. She had a court appearance today for MIT. She was a witness in a drug

30

smuggling case where she had been one of the arresting officers. She had decided to take a taxi to the High Court because parking around the Royal Mile was impossible. After going through security, Jane checked the court roll to find out where the case was being tried. They were in Court 3, in front of Lady Munro. Jane smiled and nodded. Lady Munro was a good judge. Firm but fair, was how the judge was known.

As Jane turned away from the desk, the court security guard, Imran Khan, came up to her.

"The lovely DS Renwick. Hello, my dear. Now, I hear on the grapevine that you have murderer's blood in your veins. What do you think of that?"

"I think you shouldn't believe all you read in the papers, Imran. Talking out of your arse should be avoided too."

"Ooh, that's not nice, DS Renwick."

"Neither are you. Do we have all the witnesses for our case?" she asked, deciding a change of subject would be her best course of action. Imran was a good guy, just a bit garrulous.

"We've got you and that wee black woman from MIT…"

"Do you mean my superior officer, DI Regina Jallow?"

"Aye. Feisty wee thing, she is."

"Are the civilians here?"

"Still waiting on the young lad. But he's being brought in from HMP Edinburgh, so he'll no' have any choice but to come. The old wifey is here. Right excited she is. Says she's the main witness."

"Hmm, she is certainly very important."

"She says you've no case without her."

"What's that? Oh yes, it's Imran talking out of his arse again."

"That's enough from you. Go and get a seat til you're called, DS Renwick." Imran winked at Jane. She shook her head and went to find Regina.

***

"DS Renwick, how are you bearing up?"

"Fair to hellish, boss."

"Still puts you ahead of the crowd."

"Sadly yes."

"Do you think we'll get Connor O'Grady nailed this time?"

"I hope to God we do. But I'm not sure it matters what we say. His brief will claim we are being vindictive in respect of their law-abiding businessman client. What really matters is what old Mrs Jenkins says."

"Is she the waitress?"

Regina nodded. "She's worked at The All-Day Breakfast Café since God was a boy. In fact, I think she may have served the Good Lord's father personally."

"Has she been in a safe house?"

"No, wouldn't go. We've had officers with her round the clock, partly to keep her safe, partly to prevent her from going to work while the case was being prepared. She suffers from verbal diarrhoea and would be bound to say something out of turn to one of the customers."

Jane smiled. "I bet that posting was a little slice of heaven."

"I'm glad I didn't have to do it, that's for sure. Oh, look Jane, you're on. See you later."

Jane gave her evidence succinctly and left the courtroom as Regina was called to the stand. She waited outside and hoped the senior officer would make time to go for a coffee with her afterwards.

As it was when Regina came out, she gave Jane a big smile.

"Lady Munro has called lunch half an hour early. Shall we go and get a bite to eat and stop on to listen to Mrs Jenkins damn O'Grady for trying to enlist her regulars into his web of vice?"

"Sounds good. Do you just want to go to the cafeteria?"

"Indeed I do not! I took the liberty of phoning Deacon Brodies. I got the last table. We'll have nae view, but we'll eat properly. My treat."

"Thanks, boss. That would be really nice."

They climbed the back stairs to the popular city centre pub and were shown to a small table in the middle of the room. Regina chose the fish and chips, but Jane had a superfoods salad, without dressing.

"So that's how you keep that fine figure of yours. Well, I'm not giving up my chips for anybody."

Jane smiled. "Did DCI Mackay show you what was found on my brothers?"

"Yes, he did. It's good work that was done so much more quickly than we expected. But I must tell you, they are all keeping well below the radar."

"If you had come from my family, you would too. Not claiming benefits, then?"

"Not under their birth names in Scotland. We're now looking for tax records for paid work. It's an uphill struggle, but we'll get there. I just hope they haven't changed their names."

"I hope not too," Jane said sourly.

Their meals arrived and they tucked in hungrily.

"I'll look through the old newspapers next and see what I can find."

"Craig had a couple of run-ins with us as a juvenile, but nothing since. We found a Donald Smith who was in Shotts high security prison for long and weary."

Jane raised her eyebrows.

"I don't think it's your relative, though. This one killed his ex-girlfriend and the baby she was carrying with her new partner. Claimed it was an act of God, he said, as the partner was black."

"Fucksake. No God I heard of would want a baby to die because of that," Jane stared at the remnants of her meal. Then she asked, "What happened?"

"His brief got it down from murder to manslaughter. He's been such a good boy he's in the open prison at Castle Douglas now."

"Jesus! That doesn't sound like the Donny I remember. Of course, he was only seven."

"Yep, and you were five. Not a good guide. You finished? We've just got time to visit the ladies' room before we get back to work."

"Thanks for lunch, boss. That was kind of you."

"My pleasure girl. Let's go."

33

The detectives slipped into the back of the court room and took their seats. When Lady Munro entered, everybody in the room rose and bowed in acknowledgement, then sat immediately after the judge took her seat.

They watched as she adjusted the papers in front of her and then whispered softly to the clerk of court. The judge nodded and signalled for the next prosecution witness to be brought in.

Jane and Regina saw Mrs Jenkins bustle to the front of the courtroom in her smart coat and flat shoes. The woman took her place in the witness box, had a good look around and smiled warmly at the judge.

"Hello, dear," the old woman said. "You've done well for yourself."

They found it difficult not to laugh, but Lady Munro ignored the remark and asked the clerk to help the witness take the oath or affirm if she preferred.

"Do you want to swear or affirm, Mrs Jenkins?"

"What's that, son? I dinnae swear."

"You'd rather affirm then?"

"You'll need to speak up, laddie," she said to the clerk. Jane thought him a bit old to be described as a 'laddie'. The man looked sixty, if he was a day.

The clerk raised his voice and again asked Mrs Jenkins whether she wanted to swear an oath to God to tell the truth or if she would prefer to promise to do so.

"Can you no' come a bit closer, I just cannae hear you right."

Regina and Jane were aghast. The woman was as deaf as a post. It took the clerk standing right in front of her and Mrs Jenkins coming down out of the witness box before she grasped what he wanted her to do.

Then the prosecutor stood up.

"Mrs Jenkins, do you work at the All-Day Breakfast Café in Clerk Street?"

"What's that? Oh, the All-Day Breakfast? Well, I work there, son. Have done for years." She adjusted her bosom through her coat.

Mrs Jenkins reminded Jane of the late comedian, Les Dawson. She giggled. Lady Munro frowned.

"Did you overhear the accused approach some of your regular customers to join in his nefarious activities?"

"What's that? I cannae hear you. You'll need to come closer."

The prosecutor asked the judge's permission to step forward and this was granted. "Do you have a hearing aid, Mrs Jenkins?" he asked.

"No, not at all. They're for old folks."

Everyone in the court room laughed, even Lady Munro.

"How close were you to the accused when you heard him speak to your regular customers?"

"Can you speak up, man? Can I get down out of here to stand closer to you?" she asked the prosecutor.

"My Lady?" He looked wearily at Lady Munro.

"Give it a try," the judge said.

The witness and prosecutor stood no more than three feet apart. He repeated his question.

"He was in the booth, and I was behind the counter, so about as far as I am from the first row of seats over there, and I heard every word he said. Of course, wee Sally and Big Ronnie told me all about it anyway, so I know what he said."

"But what did you hear him say?" the prosecutor shouted.

"Wee Sally said..."

"No that's hearsay. Tell the court what *you* heard, Mrs Jenkins."

"But Big Ronnie told me..."

"No what did *you* hear?" the prosecutor asked again.

O'Grady's advocate had heard enough. "My lady, may I ask my client to count to ten in a normal voice and miss out one number. Then perhaps the witness could confirm the number omitted."

Lady Munro agreed and the process was explained to Mrs Jenkins by the clerk standing near her.

Jane and Regina watched as Connor O'Grady stayed sitting and heard him count to ten, omitting the number seven.

Mrs Jenkins stared at him.

"Well?" asked the clerk.

"I'm waiting for him to speak."

"He did."

"Get him to stand up, I didn't hear that."

"Was he standing up in the café?" the defence advocate all but shouted.

"No. Why would he be?" Mrs Jenkins scowled.

"Mr O'Grady, please would you stand up and repeat the exercise?" Lady Munro asked.

O'Grady obliged. This time he missed out the number four.

"Mrs Jenkins, which number did Mr O'Grady miss out this time?" the judge asked.

"I don't know. it's too noisy in here."

"My Lady, I would venture to suggest it is quieter in here than it is in most cafés," O'Grady's advocate said.

"Most cafes are not relevant, only the one in which Mrs Jenkins works concerns us," the judge said. I call for complete silence in the court while I impose upon Mr O'Grady to do the same again. Mr O'Grady, please go ahead."

O'Grady stood and counted to ten. Again, he missed out the number four.

"Which number did Mr O'Grady omit from the sequence, Mrs Jenkins?"

"I didn't hear him, son," Mrs Jenkins whispered. "Can I no' just tell you what wee Sally and Big Ronnie tellt me?"

"I'm sorry, Mrs Jenkins, that is hearsay and cannot be accepted by this court." Lady Munro looked at the prosecutor.

He stood up and said wearily, "My Lady, the prosecution has insufficient evidence to proceed with this case against Mr Connor O'Grady. I would be grateful if you would permit the case against him to be dismissed."

The case against O'Grady was accordingly dismissed and the man was hustled away by a red-topped newspaper to enable him to give his exclusive story to their readers.

The prosecutor gathered his papers and stormed out of the court. Jane and Regina were in his line of sight. "You two. Outside. Now!" he shouted.

Chapter Eight

"Have we got that warrant yet?" Amar asked Angus.

"Like I'm going to be in that chain. I don't know. I'll go and speak to DCI Mackay."

"I looked into his office. He's not here. Try DI Jallow."

"Which one is he?"

"She's the short one sitting on the desk over there."

Angus looked across at the DI and went to introduce himself. She didn't move. Nor did she stop giving the instructions to the bewildered DC she was talking to. Angus felt a bit awkward. After what felt like an age, she turned to him.

"What can I do for you, gingernut?" she asked. "And don't ask me anything difficult because I've just finished having my balls chewed yesterday by the prosecutor in the Connor O'Grady case. When I find out who prepped our main witness, Mrs Jenkins, I'll boil them down for glue. Now, what do you want?"

"I'm sorry, boss, but if I referred to your African heritage, I would, rightly, be disciplined. Please don't make fun of my Highland heritage."

"Well said, you. I apologise. That's how tender I'm feeling after yesterday." The woman slipped off the desk.

Angus realised why Amar had referred to her as short. He judged the DI could not be more than five feet three inches tall. Her tight dark curls framed a serious face dominated by intelligent dark eyes.

"Nobody else has had the guts to take me up on that. I'm impressed. What's your name?"

"Angus, boss. Angus McKenzie."

She held out her hand to shake. "Regina Jallow. You came to us from Edinburgh, Angus. Did you ever come across

Winston Zewedu?"

"Bear, yes I worked with him. But he's a rubbish footballer. Keeps forgetting he can't catch the ball and run with it." Angus grinned.

"Good rugby player though. He's got a pal, another mountain of a man, they play rugby together. Do you play?"

"No, I'm not heavy enough, or fast enough." Angus paused. "Soccer and golf. Those are my sports. I play a bit of squash and tennis too. But what I really came over for was to check if the warrant has come in to allow us to go through Zelay Sheptytsky's computer entries. Have you seen it, boss?"

"I haven't looked. If it's come in, it would be with DCI Mackay."

"That's what I thought. But he's not in today."

"It's not like him. Okay, well let's go and look at the gubbins on his desk." Angus followed the DI and thought he would enjoy working with her, as long as he took small enough steps so that he didn't trip over her. He stood in the doorway as she went through the mail on the desk. "I don't see it."

"Don't see what, DI Jallow?" Mackay said as he walked into the room. "Excuse me, Angus. Let me see if I can assist the DI."

"Morning, sir. You probably can, I was just checking if that warrant was in this morning. Have you seen it?"

"That's why I'm late, I have it here." Mackay held up the paper triumphantly.

"Excellent, sir. Are you okay for Amar and me to take it through to Edinburgh and get started?"

"Yes, indeed. Will the two of you be enough to get onto that?"

"Perhaps. We can see what is there, and then let you know."

"You do that. Now, Jallow, you have a seat, and we can go over who's doing what and the progress they are making."

***

Angus and Amar drove through to Edinburgh almost in

silence. It was not an awkward silence. They just didn't have anything to say to one another. Amar pulled up as near as he could get to the office in George Square. And they walked, in step, towards the entrance.

"It's a pity so many of the old buildings here were pulled down," Angus said.

"Yes, especially to be replaced by these ghastly concrete blocks," Amar agreed.

"I think before we go back, it might be nice to catch up with DS Renwick."

"Catch up? We only saw her yesterday. I don't think so." Amar reached the door first and yanked it open. "In fact, the more I think about it, the less I like that idea. I really don't like it."

"I think I've worked that out all by myself. No need to labour the point." Angus turned away from Amar to speak to the receptionist. We have a warrant to download Dr. Zelay Sheptytsky's entries on his computer."

"Oh, my goodness. I've never heard of this before. Do you know the professor is dead? He was murdered earlier this week and there are no classes here. Oh, Dr Pearson, I'm so glad you're here. These people want to download the professor's work. I don't know what to do."

Amar and Angus turned round and saw Gillian Pearson approaching the reception desk. Amar noticed the green flash in the front of her hair. Angus noticed the dark rings under her eyes. He guessed she hadn't slept much.

"Gillian, it's good to see you. How are you coping?" he asked. He held his arms open, and the woman moved towards him to receive a hug.

"It's so awful. He would never hurt anyone. Why did it happen?" Tears began to dribble down her cheeks.

"That's what we need to find out, for his friends and his family," Amar said. Neither Angus nor Gillian appeared to hear him.

"We'll get the bastard. Have you seen Jane?" Angus asked.

"No. Rachael phoned Tim this morning because Jane is in a bad way. Why don't you pop in to see her when you're finished here?"

"I think I may do that."

"I don't think we'll have time. Are you going to introduce me to your friend, Angus?" Amar asked.

Angus introduced Amar to Gillian, but she continued their discussion with her arm linked through Angus's.

"Nice hair," Amar said. "I've always liked the colour green, and that bright flash of colour emphasises the colour of your eyes."

"Thanks," Gillian said.

"Stop flirting, Amar. She's taken." Angus grinned. He turned to Gillian. "We have a warrant to allow us to go through the professor's computer entries and download them so we can examine his e-mails and memos that might help us identify the killer. I know it's horrible, but it will really help us. Can you give us access to his room, or do we need to speak to the vice-chancellor?"

"I can let you in. DCI Mackay phoned the high heed yins and got clearance for me to let you in. How is Allan?"

"The DCI? Grumpy as ever, especially furious that this monster managed to kill again."

"Horrible, isn't it? Come on, I'll take you to Zelay's room." They walked along the corridor, arm-in-arm, chatting, with Amar trailing behind them. Gillian paused outside the door.

"You don't have to come in, Gillian."

"The vice-chancellor doesn't want me to leave you alone, but I don't know if I can cope with being inside. There are still stains on the carpet and splatters of blood on the walls and all over his books. It breaks my heart to think of him bleeding to death."

"If it helps, he would have lost consciousness almost immediately and died within minutes. This murderer slices the carotid artery on the neck precisely with a fiendishly sharp knife. Zelay would hardly have been aware of what was going on and he wouldn't have suffered."

Gillian looked up at Angus and he saw her try to swallow hard, but without success. She turned her head away and vomited all over the hallway.

40

"At least the floor is vinyl out here," Amar said, sourly.

"Can you go and get us each a can of cola?" Angus asked. "We passed a machine in the entrance area."

"Why me?"

"Why not? Gillian, you go and clean up. I'll stay here. I promise we won't enter the room until you get back." Angus saw Gillian nod and walk towards the ladies' room with her hand over her mouth.

"What's up between you and the good doctor?" Amar asked.

"I told you. I play squash with her boyfriend."

"Looks like you want to play more than squash with her, if you ask me."

"I didn't. Aren't you getting the drinks?"

Amar wandered back towards the entrance. He chose the drinks and told the receptionist someone would need to clean up outside the professor's room."

"Christ, not again," she exclaimed.

***

When Gillian came back, Angus was still standing at the door and Amar was walking towards her. He handed her a cola. They all opened the tins and drank before Angus glanced at Gillian.

"I think we need to go in."

"I know. I'm just going to stand in the doorway. That means I'm doing what the vice-chancellor asked me and not leaving you alone, but I'm not going into the room either. I don't think I could stand to be in there, knowing what happened."

"No problem. Amar, will you wedge the door open so Gillian can see what we're doing?"

"Me again? I'm not your fucking gopher, Angus."

Angus ignored the complaint and walked towards the desk. Zelay's chair had been removed by the crime scene investigators. He looked around the room but couldn't see anything that he could sit on.

"Are there a couple of chairs in another room that Amar and

I could use?"

"Yes, there's a few in that room. It's used for seminars." Gillian pointed across the hallway.

"I'll get them. Do you want to sit too? You look a bit unsteady?"

"That might be a good idea. I feel a bit wobbly." She smiled at Angus.

When they were all seated, Amar switched on the computer and began the search.

"All we have to do is download the professor's work and emails over the last three months. We don't have to analyse anything right now, so it should be relatively quick."

"Yes, that's true," Angus replied.

"Oh, this is interesting. He's got three e-mail addresses, the university one, a personal one and this one." Amar pointed at the screen. "It's quite anonymous. No way you would realise it was him. I wonder why he had this?"

"We don't need to know. We just need to download it."

"Aren't you curious?"

"Is that his Sam Booka one?" Gillian asked.

"Yes, why did he have that?"

"He said it was just a joke one that he used for people who wouldn't learn to pronounce his name properly. I don't know if he even ever used it"

"Hmm. Let's see." Amar opened the address. "Empty inbox, no files but lots in the spam and trash. Strange. Very strange, I wonder if he was hiding something?"

"Just close it and download it like the others. We don't need to worry Gillian with this."

"Thank you, Angus. Will you boys have time for a late lunch before you go back?"

"Yes, we will, won't we, Amar?"

"Great. There's a little pub on the main road. 56 North. They serve good food too. It's a short walk. I'll take you there," Gillian said.

"You don't need to treat," Angus said.

"Tim's treat," she waved a Black American Express card above her head. "I'll book a table for 3pm. You should be finished by then and I'll see if Jane and Rachael can join us. I think they could do with the distraction."

"Good idea," Angus said.

"I don't think that's wise," Amar said. He knew he was defeated but wanted to raise his objection to the plan.

Chapter Nine

"What the hell will we do now?" Jane asked as she poured herself another coffee. "I can't sit at home and watch daytime TV all day. It'll drive me mad."

"I'm going to enjoy my day off by spending it with you. I might even curl up and finish that book I'm reading. It's the new one by Katharine Johnson. I love her novels."

"Rache, I do not want to spend my gardening leave reading fucking books."

"Well, why don't we go down to the National Gallery of Modern Art?" Rachael would have been hard pushed to think of anywhere she would less like to go, however, she was willing to sacrifice her sanity for Jane. "You like it there, and we could have a nice wee lunch at the café and then take a walk in the grounds. The trees are beautiful." This at least was true. The café did great homemade bread and soup at lunchtime and the trees outside the gallery were awesome.

"I suppose. But you can't stand the art in there."

"True, but I love you, and I'm willing to suffer it, even at the expense of not reading my book." Rachael smiled. "Is that my phone or yours? It's mine. It's Gillian. Hello, what can I do for you?" She asked brightly. "Oh, now that might be nice. We had just made other plans, but Janey might prefer this." She put the phone to her chest and turned to Jane. "That's Gillian suggesting we join her and Angus and some other guy whose name I didn't catch, for a late lunch at Fifty-six North. It means we'll have to leave the gallery for another day, but what do you think?"

"You'll be inconsolable about missing out on your modern art fix."

"I'll try to be brave. What do you want to do?"

"Tell Gillian yes. We can walk over there; it'll do me good to see other people."

"Thanks, Gillian. We'll see you there. What time? Three? That *is* a late lunch. Okay, see you there."

***

The women chatted as they walked. It was a decent stride from their flat in Bruntsfield to the pub in the university district of the city. But their route took them through Bruntsfield Links and across the Meadows. It may not have been the quickest way to go, but it was the prettiest.

"When will Superintendent Miller let you back?" Rachael asked.

"When the person who shares my DNA is caught or cleared, I suppose. It's awful, Rache. I feel like I'm guilty by association and I don't even know the sod. I remember Craig and Donny, but we were split up when I was only five, maybe six. Donny would have been a year or two older and Craig a couple of years younger. I remember Mum was pregnant when we got taken away. I never knew that one at all and I certainly don't know Craig or Donny now. I don't even know if they're both alive or use their birth names, I mean, I don't. It really sucks."

"I understand, but you know Miller is just making sure that there is no possibility of you being used as a 'get out of jail free card,' don't you?"

"Yes, I do. Literally! Looks like we're first here. Would you prefer to sit in an alcove or by the window, Rache?"

"Let's sit by the window. I think you could do with some sunlight to cheer you up. Shall we wait and order drinks when the others arrive?"

"Hello, hello. How are two of my favourite ladies?"

"I'd recognise that highland lilt anywhere. I'm feeling shit about getting pulled off the case. Sit down here and tell me what you've got, Angus," Jane said.

"Why don't I take a drinks order while you pair study the menu? I don't think we've met. I'm Rachael."

"Hi, Rachael. Amar. Can I help you carry those drinks?" He walked over to the bar with her.

"How do you like working with Angus?"

"We're still getting to know each other. But I can't say I agreed to this meeting. I think it could just give DS Renwick false hope that she may be involved in this case in some way. And she just can't."

"She knows that, but she's not good at being cut out of the loop, Amar. It'll be okay. You'll see." Rachael looked around at Jane and saw her smiling. She gave her a wee wave and ordered a coffee and a tea for the boys, three large white wines for the girls and a pitcher of tap water for the table.

"Are you ready to order?" the barman asked.

"I'll check," Amar said. When he came back, he smiled. "Easiest order in the world. One halloumi and chips and the rest fish and chips, and whatever you want, Rachael."

"Make it four fish and chips. Thanks." Rachael paid for the meals on her credit card and hoped Jane would offer to split the bill later.

When she and Amar got back to the table, Jane was listening carefully to Angus, but Rachael soon realised he wasn't telling her anything that she didn't already know.

Gillian looked up. "Rache, did you pay for lunch? I was going to make it a treat from Tim."

"My pleasure. Tim can pick up the tab next time. We'll make sure to go to the Dome or Tiger Lily's for dinner that time." Rachael smiled and poured everybody a glass of water.

"Zelay doesn't fit the profile of the other victims, so we're going through his social media profile, emails and such to try to work out how he landed on this maniac's list," Angus continued.

"Of course." Jane nodded. "You're sure it's the same perpetrator?"

"Yes. The method is exactly the same. We're pretty sure it's even the same weapon, but forensics will hopefully confirm that."

"What does the social media tell you?"

"Nothing yet. We haven't had time to examine it. Do you

remember anything about your brothers that might help us?"

"You mean did one of them pull the wings off butterflies or strangle cats? No, there was nothing like that. We were too busy surviving our parents. I recall Donny did his best to look out for us. The neighbours were always shouting at him for raiding their bins, but he was only looking for food. Craig was little more than a baby. I remember him running around with no briefs on and getting whacked when he peed or pooped on the floor. Nobody cleaned it up. He just got hit and then we had to remember not to step in it. Donny and I used to go on the rob for nappies for him."

Rachael reached under the table to hold Jane's hand. Her eyes were full of tears. She hated it on the rare occasions when Janey spoke about her childhood. She was grateful when the meals arrived. She could focus on the freshly cooked fish and well-seasoned chips with mushy peas rather than Jane's desperate memories.

Chapter Ten

"How did it go in Edinburgh?" DCI Mackay asked.

"Okay, I think. I'm just going to give the copies we took to the computer boffins and see what they can make of them, sir." Angus paused slightly and then said to DCI Mackay, "Gillian suggested we go for a late lunch before we came back. Jane and Rachael were there."

"At best, that was unwise, Angus."

"Maybe. But I'm sure she doesn't know anything about the person who shares her DNA."

"Shall I add mindreading to your appreciable list of skills, or shall I instruct that such contact does not recur? You do realise that if our perpetrator found out investigating officers had been in contact with his family, it could adversely affect our case? Do you want to be responsible for that?"

"Of course not, sir. But…"

"No buts. Just don't have any unauthorised contact with anyone, but especially not with DS Jane Renwick. Understood?"

"Understood, sir. I think Zelay is an odd one though. He just doesn't fit the profile of the other victims. Amar agrees with me."

"It's true, and Amar has good instincts. But as far as I can see, the only thing the three victims have in common is that they were born abroad."

"That's all we could get too. Shall we go over the other victims' social media again?"

"Yes. See it the professional contacts include an e-mail address. That might give us something, Angus."

"We thought so too, sir. We'll have another look."

***

Angus wandered back through to find Amar away from his desk. When he began tidying his own desk, he noticed that the USB stick containing the copies of Zelay's work and emails was not there either.

"Do you know where Amar has gone?" he asked Amar's confidante, DC Judy Marsh.

"He's taken the copies he got from Edinburgh to the forensic computer guys. He said it didn't need both of you to take it along."

"He went, and he'll take all the glory. Great!"

"Don't be so sarcastic. There's no glory in taking a few copies of anything. The glory is in catching the perpetrator."

"Judy's right, Angus. Ignore the slight, and find the proof to catch a killer for me." Angus became aware that, when standing, DI Regina Jallow was only a little taller than he was sitting down.

"You got it, boss," he said. "I'm going to go through the social media accounts for the other victims again."

He started by noting down all the Facebook pages the women had liked. Unsurprisingly, the dress designer, Dolores Cline, had taken an interest in those models who showed off her clothes at fashion shows and stores that stocked them. Angus noticed that she also liked the fashionable hairdresser in George Street, a cleaning firm charging up-market prices, a dog grooming parlour in the New Town, and the dating website he and Amar had noticed before, *Alone in a Crowd*. He wondered if she had made any connections through the website or just browsed.

The poet, Beatrice Dalgleish, had far fewer pages of interest. Angus decided that Dolores was probably the more flamboyant of the two and thought that poets would generally be less likely to be extrovert that designers. Not that he knew any designers, or poets for that matter.

There were four pages that the two women had in common: the hairdresser, the cleaners, the dog groomers, and *Alone in a Crowd*. Angus frowned as he struggled to decide whether to

49

get himself a coffee before or after checking Zelay's likes.

"Tea, Angus?" Amar asked.

"Coffee please. Just milk."

"I hope you don't mind me slipping along to forensics with the finds while you were in with Mackay."

"Why should I? No kudos in copying things. That only comes when we nail the bugger."

"What you doing now?"

"I'll show you once you're back with my coffee."

Angus watched Amar walk away and felt a pat on his shoulder. "You're getting the hang of him, lad. Don't let him sway you off course." Regina whispered in his ear.

It did not surprise Angus that Zelay had fewer liked pages even than Beatrice. He could imagine the academic as a most serious-minded man who had lived in a rented flat, so was unlikely to have a pet. Sure enough, the dog groomer was not amongst those he followed. He worked at the university, so was unlikely to spend either the time or the money going into town to get his hair cut at the fashionable salon. Angus proved himself right again. Zelay had followed a hungarian restaurant in West Maitland Street, a polish restaurant on the east side of the city, and liked the page for the Scottish-Ukrainian Society in Edinburgh.

Amar came back and put his coffee on the desk. "What's up?" he asked.

"I'm just trying to see if there are any connections between the interests of our three victims."

"Good. What have you got?"

"All three had reading privileges at The National Library of Scotland. They have all been to garden parties at Holyrood, but not the same one and they all had season tickets to The Lyceum Theatre. None of those sound particularly threatening."

"No, they don't," Amar said.

"Apart from that, the women have a dog groomer, a hairdresser, a cleaner and a dating website in common."

"A dating website? Ooh kinky."

"It doesn't look very kinky. It is said to cater for

50

professionals leading busy lives in the modern world."

"And Zelay?"

"So far, nothing. He didn't need a dog groomer, didn't go into town to get his hair done, and having looked around his office, I think we both saw cleaning wasn't high on his list of priorities."

"Well, I don't know if he can be entirely blamed for that. Look, here is that the same dating website running the speed dating Zelay was interested in?"

"It is! We have a match."

Angus grabbed his list and strode into DCI Mackay's office.

Chapter Eleven

"How come we ended up coming back into Edinburgh for the post-mortem? Couldn't Mackay have got a couple of the local boys to do it?" Amar asked Angus. "I hate the smell of those places, and the sounds when they make the cuts into the chest and watching all the innards coming out. Oh yuck!"

Angus glanced at Amar and scrunched up his face. He could have done without his new colleague reminding him of those aspects of the post-mortem that he, too, liked least.

"If you want to call the DCI and suggest the local boys take over from us, you go ahead," Angus said.

"But I probably won't."

"Good decision," Angus said as he turned into the mortuary carpark.

"How do you know this medic then, Dr Shah?"

"Sharma. Her name is Dr Meera Sharma. She was the main pathologist while I was working in Edinburgh. She's sound. Shall we get going?"

The men got out of the car and walked in step towards the doors of the mortuary.

***

Meera and her colleague, David Murray, were the attending pathologists. They scrubbed up and disinfected their hands and then Meera made her way across to the examination room where David was waiting for her. He wheeled Zelay's body out of the fridge and transferred it to a stainless-steel table that occupied the middle of the spotlessly clean white floor. The victim was lying on his back with his arms loosely resting by his sides.

"I believe this victim is friendly with Tim Myerscough. Did you know him?"

Meera glanced at David and shook her head.

"No. I think he worked with Tim's girlfriend. He was the professor in her department."

"She must be in bits," David said.

"Absolutely. This is so vicious."

"Who do you think will attend for Police Scotland today?"

"Probably members of MIT. They'll be taking the lead in this case, don't you think?"

"Well, I hope whoever has been appointed manages a little better than some of the others and doesn't faint." David smiled.

Meera nodded, then turned her attention to the body on the table. She pointed to the livor mortis on the man's body caused by the settling of the blood. "He was definitely killed in the location he was found."

"Yes, indeed," David said. "Oh, that sounds like the boys in blue are arriving."

Angus and Amar walked towards the examination room. Angus was amazed, as always, by how much it resembled an operating theatre.

The door opened. Meera looked up. She smiled at Angus. "DC McKenzie, thank you for coming. It seems we were correct, David. It is officers from MIT. I don't think I know your colleague."

"Amar Patel." Amar held out his hand to shake hands.

Meera smiled and held up her gloved hands.

"Oh, yeh, sorry doc. I get so nervous in these places. I would happily never come here again." Amar looked at the floor, then at Meera.

"I know what you mean," she said.

"Lovely as it is to chat, we should get gowned up, Amar," Angus said. He nodded to indicate that Amar he should follow him through. "There really is a distinctive smell in here, isn't there?"

"Yes, a bit like a combination of formaldehyde, antiseptic, and industrial soap, isn't it? It's also a bit chilly. Just those few degrees below what would be considered comfortable makes all the difference."

When Angus and Amar returned to witness the postmortem, Angus commented, "This is a big room."

"Yes, I suppose it is," Meera replied. "By the time I've got my large double sinks along the wall, a metal counter to hold all the tools and the channel leading to the drain, it has to be big. It also looks a lot bigger without you officers peering over and filling up my space, DC McKenzie." Meera smiled.

"Thanks, Doctor Sharma," Angus replied with a grin.

"When you two are finished sparring with each other, can we get on?" David asked.

The two DCs moved a little further forward so they could see the body on the stainless-steel examination table below the powerful circular halogen lights which were suspended from the ceiling. Meera positioned herself on the other side of the table from the two detectives.

They watched in silence as Meera first cut away the clothes from Zelay. There were no defensive wounds on the hands or the body showing that he had had no time to put up any fight against his attacker.

"David, look at this," Meera said. "It seems like his neck was wrenched backwards swiftly and then sliced from right to left through the carotid arteries in one sure movement, but there is a second slice across the breastbone which is not nearly as deep. It's the same method used in the murders of those two women who were killed earlier in the year. In all three cases, the victim would have lost consciousness almost immediately and died within a couple of minutes, wouldn't they?"

"Might he have been throttled into unconsciousness before his neck was sliced?" David asked.

"No, I don't think so. That's not consistent with what I'm seeing. There's not the bruising or handprints on the neck, but from the injuries he sustained, I believe death would have been quick."

David pulled a face as he watched Meera finish removing the clothes to get a better look.

As each piece of clothing was taken from the body, Meera methodically gave them to David. He put each item carefully into plastic evidence bags which would be handed over to the forensics experts for further examination. Meera then took blood, urine, and hair samples, as well as oral and anal swabs.

"Is that how you get urine from a corpse?" Amar asked.

"Yes, I obtain the urine by aspiration with a syringe, without a needle, once the dome of the bladder has been opened."

"If this procedure is adopted, we have to be careful to make sure that the urine sample doesn't get contaminated in any way," David added.

"That's fascinating, and a bit gruesome," Amar said.

"I don't suppose there's much doubt about the cause of death, Meera." Angus grimaced.

"I can never be sure until I've finished the postmortem. But if I had to take a punt with that deep cut across the neck, the poor soul would have bled out from that in minutes. Zelay would never have recovered consciousness from the attack and the slicing of his throat. There wouldn't be time. Look, the injury is right across the front of the neck. It's almost like a butcher trying to behead a beast."

Amar gasped.

Angus closed his eyes.

"Monster!" David whispered. "His office must have had splatters of blood all over, and I imagine there was a large pool of blood where he died. This attack was vicious and deliberate."

"You're right, David. But why?" Angus whispered.

"Who knows. I'm glad not to be able to read the mind of the creature who did this." David turned and reached for the digital camera. He documented everything as Meera finished undressing the body and as she scraped gently underneath the nails of the fingers and ran sticky tape across Zelay's hair.

"I have fragments of skin here in the hair that might give us DNA from the attacker," she said.

She sprayed the body with fungicide and used a hose with a powerful water jet to methodically wash and disinfect the corpse fully. When she was finished, she turned on her voice recorder and dictated the official examination. She began by stating the date and time, followed by the case number then she outlined the general state of the body, before she moved on to describe the grisly details.

Meera checked that the directional light in her headset was switched on, although she knew it was, it gave her a couple of seconds to compose herself discreetly before she began precisely checking the skin around the corpse's neck.

"No other suspicious bruises, but there may be DNA on the neck," David commented.

"Possibly, but unlikely. In light of these wounds, it would appear that the weapon was a large, knife. I doubt the perpetrator touched Zelay to inflict that wound," Meera said.

"It must have been a phenomenally sharp knife," David added.

Meera nodded, then turned her attention back to the body. She checked for signs of sexual or any other kind of aggression. She began with the mouth, pulling it open and checking for any trauma or skin and teeth in case a poison had been used which discoloured the teeth or tongue, or perhaps burned the skin inside her mouth. Meera found no primary indications of poisoning, but samples would be sent for a toxicology report in any event. She and David were always thorough.

Chapter Twelve

The Superintendent of The Major Incident Team of Police Scotland held a press conference. I knew I shouldn't have gone, that it was probably a bad idea, but I couldn't resist after they put out that a DNA match had come up for the perpetrator. I sat in the front row with a notebook and pencil, scribbling like the other journalists as if my life, and job, depended on it. Of course, they didn't. I have never been a journalist, and since the accident, I haven't had much of a life either. I can't stop thinking about what happened, and how there was no justice for me and my girl.

Anyway, I've decided I won't go back into Edinburgh University. I can't risk it. I'll have to let that woman with the green hair go for now. She would have lost her life if the professor hadn't got in the way. But nobody else here knows that. How could they? I have a list and it makes sense to progress through that. I'm going to do the easiest ones first, and I've decided I'll catch her at the end.

It was funny to sit and hear the police talk about the connections between the three victims, because they didn't exist, certainly not with the man. He was just in the wrong place at the wrong time. A bit like Aqua, I suppose, and me. I was born into the wrong family, bumped from pillar to post in the care system and seven schools in four years until they found me a forever home. I'm just as clever as the professor was, I could make a name for myself. I suppose I will. The wisdom I could share would flow beautifully and contain important hints and tips for those coming after me, I'm sure. I just haven't put anything tangible together yet. Still, who in the world should judge me?

And Aqua, my little jewel. Part of my family but parted

from me by her bloody mother. Look how that turned out. She didn't even clean her teeth properly. Having to take her to the dentist at three years old? What kind of care was that? And that decision. A bloody travesty. You can believe me when I say they'll all bloody suffer, and I'll put it right.

Oops. I wrote that down. The journalist next to me was squinting at my notebook and frowning. I turned the page and smiled at her. She smiled back. I needed to listen and concentrate.

There were questions to the superintendent. 'Do they have a picture of the perpetrator?' I was surprised when they showed a photofit. I had no idea who it was meant to be, but luckily it looked nothing like me. 'Will copies of the picture be distributed amongst the press?' Good, I could pick that up on my way out. 'Do they have suspects they are questioning?' Apparently not. 'Is it true the main suspect is a relative of one of their detectives?' The superintendent makes no comment and drew the meeting to a close. He left abruptly.

"What do you think?" the journalist next to me asked.

"They don't seem to know much."

"If it's a relative of one of their own officers, that's immense."

I decided not to comment on that. What could it accomplish? Nothing good for me.

The journalist in the row behind tapped me on the shoulder. He offered a handshake. "I'm Paul Jones, from The Scotsman. Not seen you before. Which publication you with?"

I mumbled something about being an online paper.

"Which one? I used to be with HuckTimes."

"Yeh, that's it."

"Do you know Gemma Partridge?"

I ignored the question and moved away. I pushed past several other guys and got a copy of the picture.

I heard Paul mutter about me to another of the hacks. A few of them were angry that I shoved my way to the front of the line. I shouldn't have drawn attention to myself. I really shouldn't have come at all. I knew it was a bad idea, but it was irresistible to hear, first-hand, what the police were making

public, what they said about me.
    That picture really does look nothing like me.
    Result.

Chapter Thirteen

"It was nice having lunch with Gillian and the boys, wasn't it?" Rachael said. She looked at Jane and was sad to see her solemn expression. Jane liked to be in the centre of the action. It was clear to Rachael that being side-lined was tearing her apart. Rachael was desperate to stop her falling into a depression. She knew that could last for weeks. "Janey?" She sat on the sofa and looked up at Jane. She took her hands in hers and kissed them gently.

"Yes, but you and I both know Angus will get a bollocking for meeting us."

"He's a big boy. He'll cope. What did you think of Amar?"

"Alright, I suppose. He didn't say much. I'm not sure he wanted to be there. You want a tea?"

"Yes please, honey." Rachael followed Jane through to the kitchen. "I wondered if you'd like to go to the zoo tomorrow?"

"I feel a song coming on." Jane smiled. "What made you think of the zoo?"

"We haven't been for ages and the weather forecast is good enough for a long walk. We could have lunch there. I thought it might be fun."

"Am I that bad?"

Rachael nodded. "Am I that obvious?" she asked.

"I'm sorry to disappoint you, but I have other plans for tomorrow."

"Great. What are we going to do?"

"You don't have to come, but I am going to see if I can find copies of the birth certificates for my siblings. Then I'm going to try to find them on the voter's roll, or even on the last census."

"And what exactly would you plan to do with that

information, even supposing you found it? They may not still use their birth names. You don't. Do you plan to knock on the door of a triple murderer and say, 'Hello, bro, long time no see, I wonder if you killed my friend's boss'?"

"Don't be ridiculous!"

"You're the one who is going on an unauthorised man-hunt for a murderer. And you say I'm the one being ridiculous. No, Janey. We are *not* going to do that."

"True. *We* are not going to do anything. *I* am going to check the Register of Births, Marriages and Deaths tomorrow and find out what I can about my siblings. *You* can stay at home and paint your nails or wander around the zoo and have lunch or whatever you like."

"That is not fair, and I don't deserve to be spoken to like that. I'm off to spend the evening with Mum and Dad. Call me when you're ready to apologise."

Rachael grabbed her coat from the hall stand, picked up her purse, and trotted down the stairs to the street. She decided that she would take a number twenty-three bus to Trinity and walk the few blocks to her parent's house from there. She and Jane rarely argued and falling out always made them both miserable.

Her mother answered the door. "Hello, darling. Where's our favourite daughter-in-law?"

Rachael burst into tears and told her mother what had happened.

"Come in. Let's have a cup of tea. Then I'm going to take you home and you and Jane can sort this out. Never go to bed on an argument. And especially never run away to your family when she feels she doesn't have one."

"That's just the problem. It's her family, and her search for them that is causing all the trouble."

"Then you must stand by her, not run away from her. You know family is Jane's Achilles heel, and she is part of our family now. We can't allow her to hurt like this." Her mother smiled.

***

Rachael unlocked the door to the flat. Inside, it was in darkness. She switched on the living room lights and saw Jane sitting on the floor in the lotus position.

"My goodness, Jane darling," Rachael's mother said. "You must be extremely supple to do that. Now, Rachael has told me that you have some plans for tomorrow that she does not agree with. How about I make us all a cup of tea and you two can talk it through and get to some sort of agreement. It seems silly, Rachael having taken this week off to be with you and then you spend the time apart."

Rachael watched as Jane unravelled herself from the yoga pose, then stood up and went over to hug her mum.

"Of course, you're right, Mum. Rachael just drives me round the blooming bend sometimes."

"Welcome to my world, Jane. Chamomile tea for both of you? I'll have an Earl Grey if you have some. Now, talk."

Rachael sat on the sofa and her mother went next door to the kitchen.

"Did you hear us coming up the stairs?"

"Of course, like a herd of buffalo."

"What were you watching?"

"The Simpson's Movie."

"You must have been quick to get that and the lights off and into lotus before I opened the door."

"Yes, and I hadn't done any warmup, so my leg muscles are sore now." Jane massaged her thighs.

"Serves you right, you stubborn bitch."

"I suppose it does."

"Tea for three," Mum said. "Have you agreed a plan?"

"No, but I was going to suggest that we both go to examine the registers tomorrow. If we find anything, we phone Angus and he can get it into the correct channels," Rachael said. She sipped her tea and looked from her mother to Jane. "*We* don't go anywhere near the people of interest. *We* don't put ourselves into danger. But I'm coming with you."

"Because you don't trust me."

"That's true. But it's not the reason. We'll be quicker if we're both searching."

She saw Jane smile. "Okay, we'll do it your way, Rache. And thanks for your help, Mum."

"All I did was make tea. Now, I'll be on my way. I think I'll pick up fish and chips for me and your dad tonight. I can't be bothered to cook." She pulled her car keys out of her pocket, hugged, and kissed both Rachael and Jane, and walked down the stairs whistling Venus the Bringer of Peace by Holst.

"She wouldn't let me stay," Rachael said.

"I knew she wouldn't. I'm her favourite."

"She certainly says yours was the easiest birth."

Jane giggled. "She does, doesn't she?"

Rachael nodded. "Talking about eating, what do we have in the fridge?"

"Cheese and leftovers from last night, or there's some bolognese in the freezer. I could boil up some pasta. Which would you prefer?"

"Let's go with the pasta," Rachael said.

"And a good red wine."

"Agreed. Come here, you hussy. Give me a hug before you make my dinner."

"Rachael Anderson, who said I was cooking dinner?" Jane laughed. She knew she would have to look for her siblings, but that argument could wait for another day.

Chapter Fourteen

"I cannot fucking believe it. Another bloody murder. Is that right? Another one, and we're no further forward. Fuck's sake. Who is it this time? Jallow? Who's there? What do we know?" Jallow thought Mackay had turned an unhealthy red colour.

"The victim is a judge. Lives in Moray Place in the New Town. Lady Munro," she said.

"Who is at the scene?"

"Local boys. I'm waiting on a report, and there's a Doctor Sharma who will conduct the post-mortem."

"I know Meera. She's good. I'll phone her and ask that she expedite this one."

"You know her, sir?"

"Yes, I do." Mackay looked around the team. "What do we know about Lady Munro?"

"Fifty-five years old, divorced, two grown up children, appointed to the bench several years ago."

"I want you to find out everything there is to know about this bloody victim by the end of the day. Do I make myself clear?"

"Yes, sir."

"McKenzie, I want every connection between Lady Munro and the other three victims by close of business. I want to know everything, even if they use the same hair dye or breathe in the same rhythm. Do you understand?"

"They're all dead. They don't breathe at all, sir."

"Fuck off, McKenzie. Patel, I want a list of all the cases Lady Munro has presided over since she was appointed a judge. I'll get the locals to interview the ex-husband and the children."

"Do you think this death is connected with the other

murders, sir?" McKenzie asked.

"How would I fucking know? But I hope it is, otherwise we've got two bloody killers on the loose. Now, if you don't have any other idiotic questions, I'd like you to get on with your investigations." Mackay glowered at Angus and at Amar before he stormed back into his office.

***

"How on earth do I find out about the cases Lady Munro presided over, Angus?" Amar asked.

"I don't know. There must be court records that will give you the information. Maybe you could phone the High Court or Court of Session and find out. If I were still in Edinburgh, I'd ask Jane Renwick."

"Hmmm. I doubt that would go down too well. I think I'll Google it, and see how I get on from there."

"I don't blame you." Angus smiled. "Do you want a cup of tea? I'm going to make myself a coffee before I settle down."

"Yeh, go on. I can't tell you how much I hate this desk-based detection work. I'd rather be out in the streets or interviewing the family," Amar said. "Judy, could you find out about Lady Munro and her family? Why did she divorce?"

"Who made you my pimp?" Judy growled.

"Pretty please." Amar held his hands together as if in prayer.

"Go on then, arsehole."

"When did DCI Mackay say the next briefing would be?" Angus asked.

"He didn't say. My guess is he'll call it whenever he gets the post-mortem report."

"Yes, that would make sense, Judy. We better just crack on." Angus placed the mugs of tea and coffee on his and Amar's desks and started to delve into Lady Munro's social media profile.

Chapter Fifteen

"I didn't even know this was here," Rachael said as she and Jane entered New Register House in West Register Street. "I thought we'd go into that big fancy building with the dome behind the statue of the horse."

"No, that's General Register House. Public access hasn't been available for a few years. It's because there are safety issues with the Adam Dome itself."

"How come you know so much about it?"

"I phoned and asked where we should go before we left the flat."

"Very sensible of you."

"One of us has to be."

The women submitted to the security checks and Jane explained that she wanted to search for her parents' marriage certificate and her siblings birth certificates. They were directed to a desk. Jane brought out a notebook and pen. The registrar made it clear that they were not permitted to mark any of the documents nor to take photographs with mobile phones or any other copying device.

"We are both serving police officers. We're used to following rules," Jane said.

The man smiled and told them how to search the records. He made it clear he would be happy to afford them any help they needed.

"What do you want me to do first, Janey?" Rachael asked.

"I think we need to look for the marriage certificate. I was born twenty-nine years ago, and my older brother was two years older. I would guess it was pretty much a shot-gun wedding, so let's have a look for their names in the register thirty-two years ago and then work backwards."

"I'm surprised they married at all after all you told me."

"You have a point. Let's look, shall we?"

"Of course. Remind me of their names."

"I don't remember if they had middle names. I was too young to ever know."

"Won't their full names be on your birth certificate? Get it out of your bag and let's take a look. Honestly, Jane, you are meant to be the clever one of the two of us."

"I'm just so bloody tense."

"I worked that out all by myself, pet. Come on, Let's see."

"You're joking John Donald Smith and Jane Craig or Smith. Shit! Could they have had more common names? Remind me where did you get Renwick, from again."

"My last foster parents. I was with them until I turned sixteen and they offered me the chance to change my name to theirs. I jumped at it. I thought, at last, I belonged. Shortly after that, one of their friends started touching me and kissing me whenever we were alone. I couldn't cope, so I ran away. I never did tell them why.

"Anyway, that was a good thought, to look at my birth certificate. At least we know who we're searching for."

"Exactly. Aren't you glad you've got me?"

"You will never know how much, but enough of the Rachael Anderson appreciation society. Let's get on."

It didn't take long for the computerised records to show up a likely wedding match. Rachael tapped Jane's arm and pointed to her screen. Jane stood up and peered at the screen.

"Yes, that must be right, because Mum was very young."

"This couple were both incredibly young. She was only sixteen, and he was just a year older. It's no big surprise they made such a mess of things."

"I lived through it. I have no sympathy for either of them. Can you order a copy of that?"

"Of course. They married on Christmas Eve, the day after she turned sixteen."

"She was probably already pregnant, Janey."

"Yes, likely. Dad was a pest with young girls. Even me. I'd lie very still and pretend to be asleep."

"Oh, God. No!"

"I didn't want to wake wee Craig, so I'd bite my sleeve until my tongue bled. I'm pretty sure Donny knew."

"Didn't he help you?"

"What could he do? At most he was seven years old. We were all trapped in that nightmare.

If you look for Donny's birth certificate now, I'll start looking for Craig. Donny was about two years older than me, and Craig three years younger."

"I know the respective ages. You don't have to keep telling me, pet. Can you remember what time of year it was?"

"No chance. And for Craig, I can't even remember exactly how much younger than me he was."

"Is."

"What do you mean 'is'?"

"Well, unless he's dead, he still *is* younger than you by the same amount, even if you don't see him. You should say 'is' not 'was', shouldn't you?"

"That's a thought. What if he's dead?"

"Why would he be dead?"

"Well, it does happen, you know."

"Don't get huffy, Jane. Let's look for the birth certificates before wasting energy on possible deaths."

"I'm not huffy. I'm tense."

"I know, and I do understand. Let's start searching."

It didn't take Rachael long to find Donny's birth certificate. He was born less than three months after his parent's wedding on twenty-third of March but searching for Craig took longer because the only parameter the women had was Jane's date of birth. They started searching exactly a year later, but found nothing within the next five years.

"This is too far on. There's no way Craig was five years younger than me. Let's start again," Jane said.

"Oh God! I don't like to complain, but this is bloody boring."

"Thanks. I didn't think you'd last the pace."

"Oh, that's not fair. Who's that? What's he looking at? Do you know him? He keeps looking at us."

Jane looked around from the computer screen. Her glance followed Rachael's and she saw the man who had caught her attention during her run and his familiar tattoos. He was talking to the registrar but staring across at them. Jane stood up and began to walk towards him, but he seemed to finish his conversation abruptly and walked out of the door and back onto the street.

She went to the registrar. "Who was that guy who was talking to you?"

"Didn't give his name. He was asking what sort of information he could get from here. Seemed more interested in you and your friend than what I had to say."

"Why?"

"How would I know? He didn't say. Maybe he just likes a pretty face."

"Do you have CCTV here?"

"Of course. The security had a full overhaul after 9/11."

"Can I see it? I'd like a print of a picture of that man."

"Only the police can get that, and only with a warrant, I think."

"We are police," Jane said, taking out her ID. "And that man was wandering about our back garden, and he followed me when I went for a run. We are in fear for our lives. If we end up dead or harmed and you haven't allowed us to pursue him, it might be found to be your fault. Are you going to insist on a warrant?"

"When you put it like that, maybe I can help."

Jane smiled. She turned to Rachael and winked and saw Rachael look heavenwards.

"Please will you look through the records again for Craig while I look through the CCTV?"

"Of course I will. The day suddenly got much more interesting. I'm going to start from the day after your birthday and search forward. That way I can't miss him."

"I hope not. Good luck."

Jane followed the registrar towards the office that housed the CCTV.

"I take it that man hasn't been in here before."

"Not that I remember. Not when I've been on duty. He is quite striking, I'm sure I'd remember. How far back do you want me to take the tape?"

"Does it cover outside the building as well as inside?"

"It covers the street in front of the entrance, the entrance itself, and the whole of the inside of the building."

"Please show me inside of the building from the time the man came in and the outside of the building from five minutes before we came in," Jane said.

"You think he followed you here?"

"I don't know. But I want to be sure one way or the other. I want to know how much danger he might pose to us."

Jane scoured the details of the CCTV. She noticed how the man walked with an easy, swinging gait. She saw where he stood and watched as she and Rachael talked at the door of New Register House before disappearing into The Guildford Arms pub when they entered the office. The registrar stood at her shoulder and watched with her.

"Who is he?" he whispered.

"I wish I knew," Jane replied. "Could you print me a copy of that, please?"

"I shouldn't. You know, not without a warrant."

"I know, and normally I wouldn't ask, but I'm just so worried," Jane pleaded.

She saw the man press a couple of buttons and a print from the CCTV was ejected from the machine behind them.

"Don't you say where you got this from."

"I won't. I promise, thank you so much," Jane said. She thought, it's pretty bloody obvious where I got it from, he's standing at your desk in this public office. But these thoughts she kept to herself.

Jane walked back to Rachael. "What have you found?"

"I've found that you and Craig are Irish twins."

"What does that mean? I'm not Irish."

"It means you were only born ten months apart, silly."

"Oh, right. That surprises me, I remember him as being a baby, but he must have been four. Poor wee sod wasn't even potty trained. You didn't manage to find the baby mum was

70

carrying when I was taken away, did you?"

"Yes, a boy. Another full brother five and a half years younger than you. But there's an adoption certificate for him. I don't know why, but he was immediately placed with a foster family and eventually adopted by them but not until six years later."

"I wonder why. Does it give his name?"

"Troy Bean."

"What?" Jane laughed. "Troy Bean? Well, he's either going to be a victim or a bully, isn't he? Have you ordered the prints?"

"Yes, they're all ready for us to pay for and collect on our way out."

"Good. Let's pay our dues and go to get a coffee in the Café Royal."

"Good idea. Your treat. I'll have a pastry too." Rachael smiled.

Chapter Sixteen

Angus and Amar were not pleased when DCI Mackay asked them to attend the post-mortem for Lady Munro.

"But we had to endure the other one for that professor," Amar complained.

"Precisely why I want you two to attend this one and observe the similarities and differences, DC Patel," Mackay said. "You can see it makes sense."

"But…"

"No buts, Patel. Except for you two getting your butts in gear and getting over to the Edinburgh mortuary. Now."

Amar followed Angus out to the car. "Piece of shit, this is. And who made you the driver?"

"Do you remember the way to the mortuary?"

"No."

"So, I'm driving. Why are you in such a dreadful mood today? Woman trouble?" Angus asked.

"Is it that obvious?"

"Just a bit. What's up?"

"I forgot our six-month anniversary. She's been giving me grief all night. Didn't even pause for breath, never mind sleep. It's like it's a crime. I didn't even know it was a thing. Did you?"

"I'm single mate. Maybe better that way, by the sounds of it."

"That's for sure. Remind me to pick up some flowers and a bottle of plonk on the way home."

The men travelled most the way in silence but the approach through a narrow street of blackened buildings to the Edinburgh City Mortuary made Amar shudder.

"Why it this street called The Cowgate? Not many cows, I shouldn't think."

"The area gets its name from the old practice of herding cattle down the street on market days."

"Oh, I see. Today is so grey, cold, and cloudy that the street seems even darker than the last time we were here."

Angus looked along the Cowgate and thought what a canyon of a road it was. The street was narrow with only one lane of traffic passing in each direction and the pavements were not wide either. He stared at the steep gradients leading off to either side. Angus glanced at Amar and noticed he was frowning. He was probably trying to hold the contents of his stomach in place.

There was nowhere obvious to park, so Angus was glad he had brought a small car from the station pool. He lurched the steering-wheel around and Amar gripped on to the handle of the door as he swung the vehicle into the morgue car park and drew up at the rear beside the anonymous black 'private ambulances' outside the morgue.

Amar's silence throughout the journey had done nothing to make it more pleasant for Angus, but Angus understood that Amar was stressed and that attending the postmortem carried a sense of duty to the victim.

Amar entered the building in front of Angus and the two detectives went through the gowning up rituals like before.

This time, Meera was assisted by Doctor Aiden Fraser and, although many of the injuries were similar to Zelay's, there were some carpet burns to the judge's legs where she had been dragged across the floor.

"You can see these injuries were caused after death because of the lack of blood flow, but I'll check for sexual assault."

"Oh God. Sex with a dead woman?" Amar began to wretch.

"If he is going to throw up, please get him out of here," Aiden instructed Angus. "And look, Meera, there has been a second slice at the neck. The first cut is the deepest, but he definitely had a second go, just like the others from what I've read in the reports."

"Oh God," whispered Amar.

Aiden looked at him sharply.

Angus saw Amar swallow his bile and shook his head. "He'll be all right."

***

"I've got the post-mortem on the most recent death, Lady Munro. Same modus operandi as the others. Neck sliced like a butcher right across the carotid artery. But she was at home and no defensive wounds but dragged across the rug in the living room. Makes me wonder if she knew her killer. Fucksake! Does this lot never shut up?" Mackay asked Jallow.

"Not often, sir. Do you want to do the call to order, or shall I?"

"You do the honours. I want to give them the details of the post-mortem and then hear from McKenzie first. I also have some information from Jane Renwick that I will share."

"I thought she was off the case."

"She is, but she's done a bit of digging into her family history that might be useful."

"Okay," Jallow said doubtfully. Then she turned and shouted. "You lot shut the fuck up, now." She frowned and looked at each officer individually. The incessant roar reduced to a whisper as the members of the team met her glance. Only Amar was looking the other way and kept talking.

"Shut it."

"Yes, boss. Of course."

"DCI Mackay has some news for us. Over to you, sir."

"Thank you, DI Jallow. Yes, we have the post-mortem on Lady Munro. As you all know, she was found dead in the drawing room of her two-storey new Town apartment in Moray Place. There were two glasses that contained wine. Lady Munro's fingerprints, and those of one other person on the glasses and the DNA of a second person, were found on the rim one of them."

"Is it the same DNA found previously, sir?" Amar asked.

"It is, DC Patel. It's almost as if the murderer is giving us tiny clues at the site of these killings."

"Hopefully they are mistakes, and there will be more of them as he becomes more careless," Jallow said.

"That would require more murders, Jallow. I certainly don't want that," Mackay said. "The method of the murder is almost identical to the other three. A deep incision into the neck slicing the carotid artery leaving blood staining the floor, furnishings and having squirted up the walls.

"McKenzie, what links our four victims?"

"They all have reading tickets for The National Library of Scotland, they have each attended a royal garden party, but not the same one, and they had season tickets to the Royal Lyceum Theatre in Edinburgh."

"Lady Munro as well?"

"Yes, sir, from what I've been able to find so far."

"All rather dull and middle class," Mackay said.

"The only other things were that the four women seemed to go to the fancy hairdresser in George Street and that the first three had all taken a six-month membership to a dating website *Alone in a Crowd* that says it caters for busy professional people in the modern world. I don't know about Lady Munro yet."

"That sounds more promising. Focus on that, Angus. And was Zelay Scheptytsky gay?" Jallow asked.

"Not that we know, boss. Why?"

"Just find out, man."

"We will. I mean *I* will."

"How did you get on with Lady Munro's caseload, Amar?" Mackay asked.

"It's slow going," Amar said. "What a lot of cases have been heard by this judge. She became an advocate in 1985 and was appointed to the bench in 2000. Since 2007 she has only heard criminal cases, so I'm starting to make my list by going back to there."

"Fine. Just keep me in the loop, DC Patel." Mackay nodded. "I have information from DS Jane Renwick that may be of assistance to you. Her birth parents' names, and the names of her three brothers. Two of the boys were in the care system and still use the family name of Smith." Mackay heard the groan go around the room. "The youngest boy was formally adopted and took the name given to him by his adoptive family, Troy Bean."

Laughter went around the team. "Poor bloody sod," Judy

said.

"Please let him be the link so I don't have to look through all the bloody Smiths," Amar wailed.

"Why does Jane Renwick have a different name, sir?" Angus asked.

"That is not our concern, DC McKenzie," Jallow said.

"Now, McKenzie, contact this dating agency and find out more about it. Patel, you now have a list of the brother's names. Find out if they crop up in Lady Munro's cases. Marsh see what you can find out about the cases Lady Munro took on as an advocate."

"That's a bit historical, isn't it, boss?" Judy asked Jallow.

Jallow ignored her. "Harris, find out who works at that hairdresser."

"But Zelay didn't go there, boss," Brian complained.

"You and Judy seem to have mistakenly thought that I am interested in your opinions. Just get on with it. The local boys will e-mail the reports of their meetings with Lady Munro's family as soon as those have been typed up." Jallow paused. "Any questions?"

"No, boss," Angus said and sat down to continue his enquiries.

Chapter Seventeen

"What are you doing?" Rachael asked Jane.

"I'm trying to find photos of my brothers online. There are bound to be some."

"Yes, but finding a Craig or a Donald Smith isn't going to be all that easy."

"That's why I started with Troy."

"Any luck?" Rachael sat down beside Jane and looked at the screen in front of her.

"Not on Facebook. I'm going to try Twitter now."

"If he's not on Facebook, he's not going to be on Twitter, surely." Rachael continued to follow the search on the screen. "Look, there's a few, but none of them are even in Scotland, never mind Edinburgh."

"He could have moved."

"He could. Shall I look at Instagram and see if I can find a mention of any of them?"

"You do that, and I'll do this. I want to see if I can find a picture."

"You want to see if it's that guy we saw at New Register House, you mean? I'm going to make a tea before I start. Do you want one?"

"Chamomile please, pet." Jane didn't even look up. She kept on searching.

***

Rachael felt they had been inside too much of the day. She sent a text to Gillian and asked her to phone Jane to ask her out for a drink, but there was no reply. Then she sent a text to Tim. He reacted right away. Jane's phone rang almost immediately.

"No, I don't think so, but thanks," she heard Jane say. "No. Rachael and I are busy today. You know what it's like."

"Who is it, Janey?" she asked.

"It's Tim. Wants to know if we can join Gillian and himself for a drink after his shift. He says Gillian wants to go out to show off her new haircut. I said no."

"Tell him we'd love to. We'll have had enough of all this by then. Come on, Jane. Let's do it."

"Did you hear her, Tim? I thought you would. We'll see you at the Golf Tavern at six. And Tim, thank you."

***

"Good to see you, ladies." Tim Myerscough stood up and hugged first Rachael and then Jane. "How are you doing Janey?" he asked softly, patting the chair beside him. "It must be hard to be out of the loop of an investigation so close to home. It's lucky Rache has some time to take off too, so you have somebody to grumble at."

"Lucky for whom?" Rachael asked quickly. "It's all right for you. You don't have to listen to her, Tim. She sits around moping, goes for a run, and comes back sweating. And she's worried, no, she's paranoid, thinking she's being followed by a tall, tattooed stranger. Where's Gillian, anyway?"

"She's just too upset about Zelay. She can't stop crying. But you've been followed? What's been going on, Jane."

"I'll get the drinks in, you hear what Jane has to say." Rachael got up from her chair and came back with pints for herself and Tim, a large glass of white wine for Jane.

"I've got crisps and peanuts in my pocket. So, has Jane told you what's going on and how you can help?"

"Yes and no," Tim said taking his beer from her hands.

"That's about right because Janey likes to help not admit she needs help. Isn't that right, girl?"

Jane looked at the others and burst into tears. There were things she would have to tell them to allow them to understand.

Chapter Eighteen

I looked across at Rachael. She was leaning forward gazing at me expectantly. Why had I never told her all this before? Because I was ashamed. None of it was my fault, but I was the one burdened with the memory and the guilt. I could feel the tears running down my cheeks.

"Nobody wanted to sit beside me. I always smelled, my clothes were never clean and often I had lice."

"Oh, Janey," Rachael said. She held my hand.

Tim just looked at me sadly.

"I was always hungry. I would try to steal or beg something to eat from other children at snack time. But nobody wanted to share with me, I was nobody's friend. Of course, there was rarely food in the house. I remember Donny looking for money people had dropped on the ground so that he could buy a bag of chips between the three of us. It was never enough, but it was warm, and it was something."

"Fucking hell, Jane, that's grim." Tim shook his head.

"Oh Janey." Rachael said as she squeezed my hand.

"Well, would you want to be friends with the smelly girl with grubby clothes who picked up food from the abandoned trays and bins in the lunch hall? I wouldn't."

"Did you get bullied?" Tim asked.

"Certainly! I was an easy target. Looking back, I really don't blame the bullies, I blame my parents. It was their job to feed us, love us, and care for us. But I never remember getting cuddled or looked after by them. Donny did his best to look out for us, but he was only a little boy. He can't have been more than six or seven when we were taken away that night."

"It must have been terrifying for little children," Tim said.

"Oh Janey," Rachael said again. She seemed lost for words

and just squeezed my hand even tighter.

"I suppose we thought that wherever they took us, it couldn't be any worse than home."

"Were you right?" Tim asked.

"I don't know about the boys. I never saw them again. I was taken to an old woman's house, at least, she looked old to me then. She was on her own, a widow, I think. She and her husband had fostered for years, but now since his death, she only took girls.

"To me, she seemed scary, grumpy and old. But looking back on it, she did more for me in a few days than my parents had ever done.

"I remember, when she opened the door, she smiled. 'You must be Jane; I'm pleased to meet you. My name is Ada.' She took my hand and led me into the kitchen. It was clean, and it smelled of fresh bread and chicken soup. 'Let me help you on to that chair. You must be hungry after your journey, so I've made you a ham salad sandwich to go with your soup and there is a glass of milk for you as well.'

"I couldn't remember the last time I had had so much food just for me. I remember eating it as quickly as I could before she changed her mind. It gave me terrible indigestion!"

"It sounds to me like going into care was a good thing for you, Jane," Tim said.

"Sort of, but I missed the boys."

"Of course."

"I still do. I don't even know if they're alive or dead."

"Well, we know one of them is alive, we just don't know which one."

"Janey, what happened next?" Rachael asked.

"Ada took me into the bathroom. I had to take off all of my clothes and I think she just threw them away. I certainly never saw them again. She helped me get into the bathtub and the water was warm. It felt lovely. It is the first time I ever remember having a bath. There were bubbles and I felt like a princess. Ada told me to wash myself and she left me to play in the bath. I was so incredibly happy."

"That's nice to hear," Rachael said.

"Then she came back with a big fluffy towel to wrap around me. 'We'll have to do something with your hair, Jane. You have your own personal zoo up there.' She cut my hair until it was quite short. That made me cry. I liked my long hair."

I felt Rachael's tears hit my hand as she gazed at me intently. "My poor Janey," she said.

"But it got worse. She used one of those all-in-one lice treatments and covered my hair with it. She had bright yellow rubber gloves and wore those to slather the stuff all over my head. It smelt horrible and she scrunched up her nose as she did the deed. I was embarrassed and it was quite frightening. I had never even seen this old woman before and she had already thrown away my clothes, cut my hair and massaged my head with rubber gloves. It was sore when her gloves worked their way over my hair, and they made a squeaky noise from time to time. That hurt my ears as well as my head."

"On the plus side, she had fed you, bathed you in warm bubbly water and dried you in a big fluffy towel." Tim smiled.

"True. Then I had to stand in the bathroom for what felt like ages while the lice lotion worked. It was probably only ten minutes or so, but I was five, and it felt like forever. The bathroom was warm, and I was wrapped in the soft towel. I liked that. It was a long time since I had been in a warm house.

"Ada talked to me a bit, but I was too over-awed to feel chatty. Mum and Dad always told us not to say anything to anybody and not make anybody as wise as ourselves. I suppose I was a bit monosyllabic."

"That's a big word for a five-year-old," Tim joked.

I smiled at him. Tim had always been one of the good guys, rich as Croesus, but generous as they come.

"I'll get us another drink while you gather your thoughts," he said. When he came back, he asked, "So what happened next?"

"She put a collar made of kitchen towel around my neck and combed my hair, repeatedly with the finest comb I had ever seen. There were no tugs because my hair was so short, but she combed it back to front, front to back, right to left and back again. She cleaned the comb so often, I thought it might be rubbed away. Then she started again with the comb through my hair in every direction until she was sure my hair was clear."

"Janey darling, how did you feel then?" Rachael asked.

"Clean. Really clean. And my head felt fabulous. Then she washed my hair and put conditioner on it that smelled like strawberries. She made me giggle when she said that if there were any little buggers left, they'd slip off my hair in the night because they didn't like strawberries."

I smiled at the memory and noticed that Tim was smiling back. Rachael tried to smile, too, through her tears. I sipped my wine and then opened a packet of salt and vinegar crisps. The thoughts of that day kept flooding back. I sat in silence for a while and only realised I was weeping again when Rachael wiped my eyes.

"Do you remember what happened next?" Tim asked.

"Vividly," I said. "She took me into a bedroom and looked through a large pile of pyjamas until she found a pink pair that would fit me. I didn't really like pink, but they were clean and warm, and it would have been rude to say that.

"I remember she let me sit in the kitchen while she made supper. It was another bowl of the chicken soup but this time with a slice of pork pie and some baked beans and potatoes. Can you imagine, two meals in one day? When I had finished eating all that, Ada sat me on her knee and read me a story."

"I bet you even remember which one," Tim said.

"Oh yes, I do. Spot the Dog. It made me laugh and I made her read it over and over again. I think I must have fallen asleep on her lap because I don't remember going to bed. But I do remember waking up in the morning in the most comfortable bed in the world. And my head didn't feel itchy. There was nothing moving in my hair. It was heavenly."

Suddenly I felt truly exhausted.

"I'm terribly tired, Rache. Can we go home?"

"Come on. I'll walk you ladies back to your flat," Tim said.

"Oh, there's no need. It's not far," I said.

"I know, but I'd enjoy the company."

That made me laugh. I knew I was not good company.

"Also, I don't like that you've been followed, stalked, and worried by a mysterious tattooed man, Jane. It's not up for discussion. I'll walk you back to the flat. Also, I'll pick you up tomorrow morning at six and you can come running with Bear and me in the Hermitage."

He stood up from the table and saw me roll my eyes.

"I don't suppose that's up for discussion either, is it?"

"Nope." Tim towered above us as he followed Rachael and I to the door. The thin, heavily tattooed man drinking at the bar had completely escaped my notice, but Tim mentioned him as soon as we went outside. It was creepy to think he'd been so close again.

Chapter Nineteen

Mackay called the room to order. "If we could have some quiet. That includes you, Judy. Thank you. Now, several of you have been working on information gathering relating to our new victim, Lady Margaret Munro."

Angus, Amar, and Judy nodded and looked at their notes.

"The local boys interviewed the family and colleagues. Suffice to say all her colleagues were shocked to the core. I don't think for a moment we have any suspects there, but Patel, if you need any help identifying Lady Munro's cases, I have a number for her Clerk of Court. He can get you any details you need."

"Thanks, sir."

"What did we find out about the family, Marsh?" he asked Judy.

"The family, sir? Well, the divorce was certainly heated at times. Even the ex-husband acknowledged that to the interviewing officers. But there were never any threats of violence nor any violence from either party during the marriage. He is a consultant neurosurgeon, and when she became a judge, they just never saw anything of one another. Apparently the arguments were all about pensions and investments, but that was all settled by the time the divorce went through. That was four years ago now."

"What about the children, sir?" Angus asked.

"The daughter is a highflyer working in the PR department of British Gas in London. The son is doing a PhD in Artificial Intelligence at the University of Edinburgh. He lives with his father in Ann Street."

"Ooh, very nice," Angus said. "That's a right posh street."

"Apparently so, McKenzie. The children have strong

relationships with both parents and are on good terms with them. Now, what did you find out about Lady Munro's social media presence?"

"As you might expect of a senior judge, she didn't have a public presence on Facebook, nor did she share photos on Instagram," Amar said.

"Quite. Did you find anything, McKenzie?" Mackay asked.

"The court puts out a court circular every week with forthcoming attractions, I mean upcoming cases. Lady Munro also had a presence on Twitter detailing her charity work for the Cat Protection League and the Scottish Society for the Protection of Children. Apart from that, there's nothing much."

"Patel, what did you find?"

"I was looking into the cases she has adjudicated, but it was slow going, sir. I'll contact her clerk as you suggest and see what help he can give."

Mackay nodded. "Judy what about you?"

"I contacted the places the other victims had in common. She used the same hairdresser as the other female victims, but that's not very surprising It is a high-end salon. She didn't have a dog, so no crossover with the dog groomer, but she did use the same cleaning firm as the other women. It has a reputation for being expensive and discrete, but when I told them why I was phoning they would only confirm the judge was one of their clients. The dating agency wouldn't budge. They said if we wanted any information. They'd have to see a warrant."

"I can't think that will be too much of a problem with a senior judge being a victim. Jallow, can I leave that with you?"

"Yes, sir."

"We'll reconvene tomorrow to discuss progress and I think I'll need to hold another press conference soon too. Briefing at eight, press conference at ten the tomorrow morning, Jallow?"

"No problem, sir. I'll arrange that."

Chapter Twenty

Mackay looked at Jallow. "Regina, you have a louder voice than me. Call these buggers to order, will you?

The woman bellowed an abrupt command and silence fell upon the team.

"I must learn to do that. You're magnificent." Mackay smiled.

"Thank you, sir. I aim to please."

"Now let's go over what we have. Four victims. Three are high profile women in the city all in their fifties and sixties, and we have a thirty-eight-year-old academic man that nobody has ever heard of, and whose name nobody can pronounce. Is that about right?"

"It would appear so, sir," Regina said.

"We have DNA evidence at the site of three of the murders to link the victims to a close male relative of DS Renwick's, a brother, I think forensics said. Is there anything else the victims all have in common, DC McKenzie?"

"The only thing all of them have in common is the method of the murder and a season ticket to the Royal Lyceum Theatre in Edinburgh, sir."

"None of the plays can have been *that* bad," Brian Harris joked.

"Did any of the victims review any of the plays on social media?" Regina asked.

"No, boss. There's nothing like that," Angus said.

"So, Brian is talking nonsense again."

"Is there anything most of the victims have in common then?" Mackay asked.

"Well, they were all on social media to a greater or lesser extent. Dolores Cline and Beatrice Dalgleish mostly promoted their work, but they also used it privately, and subscribed to a dating website that purports to be up market."

"That makes sense," Judy commented.

"The professor seemed to use it mostly to try to inspire his students, but he was also involved with the same dating website, *Alone in a Crowd*, although he appears only to have used it once for a speed dating event." Amar said. "I take it that didn't go too well, because he cancelled his membership shortly afterwards."

"What about the judge?" Regina asked.

"Cases she was hearing were documented on a court website, so she didn't use much social media for business purposes, except on Twitter if she were attending a conference or speaking at a charity event. She seems to have 'liked' the hairdresser that she and the other female victims went to and The Cat Protection League as well as the Lyceum Theatre, but that's about it. Otherwise, she used it sparingly and very privately for the occasional point of interest with her family," Amar said.

"But when the local boys interviewed the kids, they seemed to indicate most communication with their mother was through a private WhatsApp group," Angus added. "Do we have any fingerprints that might tell us which of Jane's brothers we're looking for, sir?"

"No, Angus. We don't even know if they all use their birth names. The youngest one, Troy Bean," Mackay paused to allow a snigger to work its way around the room. "Yes, I know, poor sod, is the only person of that name in the UK."

"Surprise, surprise," Brian said.

"Yes. He seems to be registered as a medical student at Glasgow University."

"We shouldn't have any trouble finding him, then," Angus said.

"The two older boys were fostered together when the kids were removed from their parents. The birth names were Donald Smith and Craig Smith," Mackay said.

A groan went around the room.

"Exactly. We need to find out where they are now, what

names they are using and what they are doing."

"When's our next briefing, sir?" Regina asked.

"Tomorrow morning, ten o'clock sharp. Get me all the information you can before then, team. Angus, you and Amar see if you can find Troy and interview him."

"Yes, sir."

"I suppose a medical student would know where to cut somebody to kill them quickly," Amar said quietly.

Chapter Twenty-One

Amar insisted on driving from the MIT base at Gartcosh to Glasgow University. He knew the area well and was pleased when the Scottish Crime Campus opened in Gartcosh a couple of years before. It was only a few miles from Glasgow. It was also only a mile or so away from his home in Coatbridge. That made a short commute to work for him, but he thought it must be a real haul for Angus to have to drive through from Edinburgh every day, but the highlander didn't seem to be phased by the journey. Neither did Jane Renwick, now he thought about it.

He was still angry with Angus for involving him in that meal with Jane and his other Edinburgh friends. It wasn't right. Also, he had driven on all their journeys to Edinburgh, although he had to admit his new partner knew the capital city much better than he did. It was probably a man thing. He knew that he much preferred to be in the driving seat than sitting as a passenger and on this trip to Glasgow he could reasonably argue that, on this occasion, he knew their destination better than Angus.

"So where is the medical school in Glasgow?" Angus asked.

"They put together a sort of medical college that includes the doctors and vets and so on a few years ago. Glasgow University has a great reputation for medicine," Amar said proudly. "My young brother is studying there. He's the brains of the family."

"Clearly he is. Edinburgh has an excellent medical school too, you know."

"Aye."

"Never mind the east-west divide, you still haven't told me

where we're going."

"I was getting to that. The new medical college is a wee bit north and west of the Kingston Bridge."

"I know that bit of the city," Angus said.

"So, from here it's not far, we'll just follow this road south and we'll be there in good time."

"When are we meeting him?"

"He said he's got a break between ten and lunchtime today. He sounded pretty curious about why we wanted to see him, but I didn't say too much on the phone." Amar indicated to turn onto University Avenue. "I didn't want to scare him off."

"Has anybody told Jane we've found one of her brothers?"

"I doubt it. She's not involved in the case anymore, remember?"

"But he's her *brother!*"

***

The detectives pulled up in the carpark and marched towards the modern building in front of them.

"Where are we meeting him?" Angus asked.

"He suggested the cafeteria, so he can use the wi-fi until we get there, and we can all have a coffee. I think, as he's a student, we'll be buying."

The building was well signposted, and Angus and Amar followed the smell of coffee and fried food until they found the cafeteria. It was busy. They went up to the cashier and asked if she knew a medical student by the name of Troy Bean.

"Everybody knows Beanie. One of the nicest lads on campus. Very quiet. Keeps himself to himself but everybody likes him. He's over there, see him? He's sitting on his own with his wee beanie hat on, pouring over that laptop as usual. Hard worker, Beanie is."

"I think you'll find his 'wee beanie' is better known as a Yarmulka," Angus said sourly.

"Oh yeh, he maybe said that. Anyway, he's over there."

The detectives thanked her and walked across the room

weaving in and out around the tables and dodging students with coffees and trays until they reached Troy. He looked up.

"You must be DC Patel." He shook hands with Amar and waited to be introduced to Angus.

"Troy Bean?" Amar watched while the student nodded and smiled. "This is my colleague, DC Angus McKenzie. We're hoping you might be able to help us with an enquiry."

"I will if I can."

"I'll get the coffees in," Angus said.

"Just black for me," Troy said. "But one of those orange and cinnamon buns wouldn't go amiss."

"No problem." Angus chuckled. "Typical student."

When he got back Amar and Troy were chatting amicably about the weather and Amar's brother who was in the same year as Troy at University. They knew each other. Angus noticed how pleased Amar was about this. He sipped his coffee and decided to move the chat to more meaningful topics.

"Troy, what do your parents do?" he asked.

"I was adopted as a boy, actually. Apparently, my birth parents were addicts. Drink and drugs, I think. I was removed almost as soon as I was born but it was a few years before I was adopted. I tried to look up my birth mother a year or so ago, but I found out she'd died of an overdose when I was ten. I haven't tried to trace my birth father. Surprisingly, they were married. I didn't think they would have been, but I haven't looked for him. I was a bit deflated when I found my mother was dead and I only have so much spare time, what with my studies and so on."

"Of course," Angus said. "Are your adoptive parents in the medical profession?"

"Sort of. Dad is a biochemist and works in a laboratory trying to find a cure for colon cancer. Mum is a nurse. They are incredibly supportive of me and my older sister."

"What does your sister do?"

"Marina's a neurosurgeon, working down at St George's in London now. She's the brains of the family. She did work up in the Royal Infirmary of Edinburgh for a few years, but she's in London now. I miss her."

Angus smiled. "I can imagine. I miss my family too. Are your parents fans of the *Stingray* puppet show?"

"Dad is," Troy smiled. "He loved all the Gerry Anderson puppet shows and even has some of the original marionettes. God help us if we ever touched those when we were kids!"

"What about your blood relatives? Do you know of any brothers or sisters that you have?"

"I've been told there were older children, but my parents said they were removed from the house due to neglect before I was even born. I guess that's why I was on the social workers' radar so early. But the family name was Smith. It's so common, I've never looked. I suppose I will one day, but my studies keep me busy."

"I can imagine. I don't blame you," Amar said.

"Anyway, what did you want to ask me about?"

Angus quietly explained the most recent murder of Lady Munro and that it was one of a series of similar killings.

Troy looked horrified. "You don't think I had anything to do with that, do you?"

"We have found DNA in relation to the cases, and it indicates the murderer is a brother of someone whose DNA we have on file," Amar said.

"Oh my God! Is one of my birth brothers a serial killer? That's horrendous. Are these the murders in Edinburgh that have been in all the papers?"

"Yes. Those are the ones."

"I'm rarely in Edinburgh, except to watch the rugby or go to a concert. Oh God this is too horrible. Thank goodness I have Marina."

"Would you be willing to give us a DNA swab?" Amar asked.

"Of course. I'll even take it myself," he said.

"And fingerprints?" Amar knew he was pushing his luck.

"If it will help."

"May we take a picture of you. There may be a family likeness that might be helpful."

"Well, as long as it doesn't get into the press or anything. I couldn't bear that. You don't really think it was me, do you? How did he kill them?"

"Perhaps we can ask about where you were on the nights in question," Angus said quietly.

While Amar took his fingerprints, he continued to ask Troy questions. he should have paid better attention to what he was doing because they smudged, and he had to do it all a second time. Still, Troy was patient and answered everything he was asked. "Can anybody confirm where you were on the nights of the murders?"

"Like I said, I was at home on those three dates, studying and then I went straight to bed."

"Nobody with you?"

"I don't look for an audience when I'm studying and as I'm single, I went to bed alone. Mores the pity. My flat mate would probably have been in, but I doubt he could confirm dates, I often spend my evenings that way."

"We can ask," Amar said flatly.

"If we need to. Your DNA and fingerprints will probably discount you," Angus said more gently.

"I know they will," Troy said. "Of course, I do. But it's still ghastly to think that such a close blood relative is a monster."

Chapter Twenty-Two

It was six thirty in the morning when DC Tim Myerscough rang Jane's doorbell.

"Madam coming running with me and the big man?" he asked.

"Well, if I'm not, I should thump you for coming around so early."

"*That* I'd like to see," DC Bear Zewedu said. He was leaning on the doorframe, grinning. "Morning, Jane. Does Rache want to join us?"

"Morning, Bear. I think that is less likely than them finding life on Uranus."

"No need to be personal."

Tim spotted the thin man he had seen in the pub the previous day as they all climbed into his car. He and Bear sat in the front. Even in his large BMW, they needed space that was comfortable. When the doors were closed, he looked at Jane through the rear-view mirror.

"Is that the guy you were approached by when you were running?"

"Where? Oh yes, that's him."

"I saw him sitting at the bar as we were leaving the pub yesterday."

"Yes, you said. I noticed him in our back green too, looking up at the flat, but when he saw me look at him, he took off."

"You know, there's a faint resemblance between the two of you," Bear said.

"Yuck. Don't say that. My tattoo is much more discreet and neither of you will ever see it."

Tim put the car in gear. He drove off while the man watched them and then jogged up the road towards the Bruntsfield Links.

"Did you hear that Angus met one of your brothers?" Tim said.

"No, I haven't heard from him for a few days. I think he gets grief from his new partner if he even mentions my name. We went out for lunch with them and Gillian, but Amar looked extremely uncomfortable. So, which one did he meet and how did that come about?"

"Unsurprisingly, it was Troy Bean. The youngest one."

"There's only one person of that name in Scotland. He wasn't exactly hard to track down," Bear added.

"I suppose not," Jane laughed.

Tim pulled up at the Morningside end of the park at Hermitage of Braid.

"Let's not discuss this in public," Tim said.

"No, best not," Jane agreed.

Tim and Bear began by warming up before they started jogging along the Braid Burn and through the Hermitage of Braid. Jane followed suit. The men had chosen to do their training on the Hermitage of Braid Circular. It was one of the prettiest paths in Edinburgh and, although they would need to run around the path several times to get their training completed, because the trail was only about two miles long. It was pretty and went along by the rippling water of the Braid Burn.

"I enjoy the sound of the river as we exercise," Tim said.

"Me too," Bear commented.

The big men had known each other since their childhood days at Merchiston Castle School and had seen each other through thick and thin. "You run between us, just in case," Tim said to Jane.

"In case of what?"

"That's right," Bear said. "Let's face it, nobody is getting through either of us to hurt you."

"I don't even know if anybody wants to hurt me."

"Maybe, but you don't stalk a police detective with good intentions."

They started running Tim in front of Jane and Bear behind her. They ran at a faster pace than she was used to. Tim noticed that when he and Bear stopped to do their burpees, star jumps and other rugby exercises, Jane just held her knees or ran slowly on the spot.

When they had finished their exercise, they jumped back into the car. "I'll take you home first, Jane," Tim said. "Bear and I can see you up to the flat. If you see that fellow again, will you call me?"

"Tim, honestly, there's no need. He might just be a weird neighbour I haven't noticed before."

"Possibly. Or he might be a weird neighbour looking to scare you or do you harm. Just phone me, will you?"

"Oh, all right. If it will make you feel better. Before we drive home, what can you tell me about this brother I've never met?"

"He's been brought up Jewish. He's a medical student at Glasgow University and, according to Angus, he seems like a decent guy. Seems he was horrified that a blood relative of his could be such a monster and he was as co-operative as could be," Bear said. "I think Angus said he even allowed them to take a photo in case the killer bears a resemblance to him."

"Ooh, that would be interesting. I must text Angus and ask him to send me a copy, when he is allowed to do that."

**

The Gartcosh team leading the investigation into the serial killer met for a briefing. It was still only eight in the morning and Mackay noticed the room stank of coffee and bacon. Did every briefing room smell the same, he wondered?

Mackay asked DI Jallow to quieten the team down. He wasn't sure how she did it, but it was one of her most disarming traits.

"Thank you," he said. "Now, I think we have news about at least one of DS Renwick's brothers, don't we, Patel?"

Amar stood up and wiped butter from his bacon roll away from his mouth with a grubby paper tissue he had in his pocket.

"Yes sir. Me and DC McKenzie went to meet with the

youngest brother, Troy Bean."

"Was he as goofy as his name?" Brian asked.

"No but he was easy to find and as helpful as possible," Angus said.

"What did you learn from him?" Mackay asked. "Anything useful?"

"His adoptive parents were up front with him and his sister, so he always knew he was adopted. He knew he was taken into care incredibly young because of the issues of neglect his older blood siblings had suffered," Amar said.

"That would include Jane Renwick, of course," Jallow said.

"Yes. But we didn't say anything about that. It's not our news to tell," Angus said. "He did try to look for his birth mother, but she had already died of a drug overdose. I don't know if Jane knows her mother is dead."

"We'll worry about that later," Mackay said. "What else did you find out from him?"

"He's a medical student. His father is a scientist of some sort," Amar said.

"Biochemist," Angus added.

Amar frowned at Angus and carried on. "His mother is a nurse, and his sister is a neurosurgeon in London. So he seemed appalled that a birth relative of his could be a serial killer when his family does so much to help people who are ill. He knows my brother. He's a medical student in Glasgow too. They're in the same year."

"That's just fine, but hardly relevant," Mackay commented.

"No, but we always have to hear about Amar's clever brother, sir. It's the law," Judy said.

"Where does this lad live?" Jallow asked, ignoring Judy's sarcastic comment.

"In a shared flat in Glasgow. Bank Street, he said. He gave us the address so we can go and question his flat mate. He's a medical student too, apparently." Amar looked up. "Do you want me to go on, boss?"

"Of course. Don't keep any secrets, you numpty."

"He let us take his fingerprints for elimination and a DNA swab."

"Good."

"We also took his photo in case there is a likeness between him and the killer. Although he's never met them, they are full brothers, so we thought there might be a resemblance."

"Good thinking, Batman," Brian said.

"That was a good idea. You got it there?" Mackay asked.

"It's on my phone," Angus said. "But I've emailed it to the lab, and we'll have prints tomorrow. Troy doesn't want us to share it though in case he is mistaken for the murderer."

"Quite understandable. So, this photo is just for internal use," Mackay muttered. "Do you think he's our man?"

"Unlikely, sir. He's studying in Glasgow. Medicine is a heavy course. He said he does visit Edinburgh occasionally to watch the rugby or go to a concert, but he denied being in the city on any of the nights we're looking at," Angus said.

Amar nodded. "I'll check his social media and we'll talk to his flatmate. But really, I don't see it being him, sir."

"Oh goody. That leaves us with the two named Smith. Fandabbydosie," Judy complained.

"Jane Renwick and her wife have been looking into the two older boys. Shall I see what she's come up with, boss?" Angus asked Jallow.

"Jane is meant to be off this case. No, Jane *is* off this case."

"Yes, boss. I believe she's using her free time to delve into her genealogy."

"Like hell she is! Still, it might give us a heads up. See what she's uncovered, Angus."

"Thank you, that's all for now folks. Keep busy. We better go and put something together for the press conference, DI Jallow," Mackay said. He led the way into his office.

Chapter Twenty-Three

I wore my old tweed jacket, well, my tweed jacket. It's not as if I have a new one, or even two. When I'd got up that morning, I'd noticed my smart trousers were grubby, so I pulled on my jeans. I didn't think to iron them, so they looked like yesterday's laundry, which they were. I saw last time that the others all wore shirts, not t-shirts, so I wore that too this time.

I moved along to the middle of a row. I'd decided to sit further back so that I was more in the centre of the pack and less obvious. There I was with my notebook and pencil, looking like every other hack in the room. And who sat beside me? That bloody chatty girl from the last time. What were the chances? I didn't need this kind of luck.

"Hello, again," she said with her smiley face and glowing skin. "Fancy meeting you here. I wonder what they'll have to tell us today. Dreadful about that judge, isn't it? In her own home. They think she let him in. Who would do that?"

"The press conference is late in getting started. I thought they said they'd kick off at ten," I said, just to have something to say.

"They're always a bit late, aren't they? So rude. As if their time was more important than ours. We've got deadlines to meet, haven't we?"

I was relieved when the police detectives walked onto the platform at this point. It meant I didn't have to make more conversation. He was a tall, middle aged man who looked exhausted. Probably hadn't slept properly for a while with all the problems that I'd given him. Of course, he doesn't know I'm the cause. The other officer was a wee black woman. I wouldn't like to get on the wrong side of her, she didn't look like she would take any nonsense. He gave a statement, and then she was in charge of permitting questions.

He told us about the killer getting into the judge's flat, but said it didn't look like a break-in. That's because it wasn't a break-in. I rang the bell and the silly cow never even looked through her spyhole to see who was there. She opened the door and turned away without looking at me chatting as if she knew me. Thank goodness for *Alone in a Crowd*.

I just shut the front door quietly behind me and followed her through to the living room. She was expecting me, well a fifty-two-year-old accountant called Clive, because there was a bottle of wine and two glasses on the table. When she finally turned round and saw me, she looked horrified.

"Why are you here? What are you doing in my home?"

"I'm the man whose wee girl was raped and murdered. You're the judge who only gave the killer five years and nine months. Five years and nine months for my wee darling's life He'll serve less than three with time off, won't he? It's not enough is it, Lady Munro? Now I'm in your house to show you what would have been fair. A life for a life. That's fair. You shouldn't have given him time off for an early plea, time off for previous good behaviour, time off for time spent on remand. He killed my wee girl and now you have to pay."

She screamed when she saw my knife, but only once. The cut wasn't quite as clean as the others. She tried to move away, but I sliced her again to be sure, just like the others. Still, the first cut was deeper. Her phone was on the table beside the bottle of wine. I picked up both, and poured myself a glass, while I went looking for her computer. I found it in a study off the hall, finished my wine and left swiftly.

The police were droning on about what a grand job they were doing and how they'd interviewed someone closely involved with the case. Apparently, they'd been helpful and opened other lines of enquiry. I smiled. I couldn't help it, there was nobody 'closely involved with the case'. I'm it. She was my wee girl and I'll get justice for her, if it's the last thing I do.

"That was interesting, wasn't it?" the female reporter said.

"Good they're making progress."

"If you say so." I turned my back on her and left the room by the opposite door. I couldn't be bothered making polite conversation anymore.

"There's something odd about him," I heard her say.

I decided there and then that I shouldn't come to anymore press conferences. But it is so interesting to hear what the police have to say about me. A difficult decision.

Chapter Twenty-Four

"Did you enjoy your run, pet?" Rachael asked.

"Yes, but those guys go at some pace. I thought I was fit, but I'm nothing compared to them."

"Well, I think you're fit, darling."

"Funny, funny. You want some?" Jane pulled a bottle of fresh orange juice from the fridge and poured a large serving into a glass.

"I've had some, thanks. Do you want the first shower? You probably need it."

"If that weren't so true it would be offensive. Do we have any muesli left?"

"Yes, and I'll put the kettle on for some tea. See you in a few minutes." Rachael busied herself in the kitchen sorting out the breakfast things and was surprised when the doorbell rang.

"Hello, Mrs Johnson. What can I do for you?"

"Oh no, dear. It's just that these were delivered to my door by mistake. I think they're really for Jane from the label. I should have brought them over last night, but I was already in my dressing-gown. I hope she won't mind."

"She won't mind at all, because we won't tell her." Rachael smiled. "I'm sorry you were inconvenienced so late, but thank you for handing them in."

"No problem at all, dear. Just wish Jane a happy birthday from me too."

"But it's not…" Rachael stopped talking when she realised the old lady couldn't hear her. She looked for a card but couldn't find one. Oh well, with so much going on, one of their friends had probably just sent them to cheer up Janey. That was nice of them.

She smiled at Jane as she wandered through drying her hair.

"These were delivered to the old dear across the landing instead of to you. Do you have a secret admirer?"

"Very secret, not even I know who it is."

"Well, you work it out while I have my shower and then we can decide how to spend our day."

***

Over breakfast, Jane told Rachael that she wanted to look for more information about her two remaining brothers.

"Do we have to? You know their names and their birthdays. Can't we just leave the rest to the MIT team?"

"You can, but I can't. Sorry, Rache."

"After all this time, there's so much turmoil. We had a nice wee life together."

"We still do. I just want to know about my birth family. Is that too much to ask?"

"No, of course not. Who were the flowers from, by the way?"

"I don't know. Mrs Johnson said there wasn't any card. It's a bit embarrassing. I don't know who to thank. I'll ask Tim. Chances are they're from him."

Rachael nodded. "So how are we going to find out about this family of yours? There are more than one hundred Donald Smiths and Craig Smiths in Scotland and twenty-four of the Donalds live in Edinburgh, but the Craigs are worse, seventy-three of them are here. I checked."

"Oh goodness. Right, let's start with the Donalds. We'll begin with the on-line people finder and see how many there are in the right age bracket."

"This is going to be a right barrel of laughs."

"You don't have to help me, then. Just piss off, Rache. I need to do this for me. If you don't want to be part of it, just bugger off."

"I'll make more tea. And I think I need chocolate." Rachael paused and then added, "Janey, we never usually argue, but since you started looking into your family, we seem to fight all the time, and I don't like it."

"I don't like it either. But this is important to me, and you don't seem to be bothered."

"I *am* bothered. If it's important to you, it's important to me. So, let's get to work."

***

The women found that of the twenty-four Donald Smiths in Edinburgh two were obviously too old, and four were clearly duplicates. That left eighteen men to search. They divided the number between them to investigate more thoroughly.

"It's amazing what you can find out about people online when you put your mind to it, isn't it?" Rachael commented. "Just by looking at the electoral rolls, I've discounted another three right away."

"Yes, I marked four off my list that way."

"Also, two of mine died young, according to the records and one hasn't been registered in Edinburgh since 2004. I'm going to see if I can find out what happened to him. Have you been able to score off anymore, Janey?"

"Like you, two deaths. Another one wasn't an obvious duplicate, but it looks like he divorced and re-married, so the address has changed as have the names of those he's living with."

"You do realise we won't get hold of the homeless or those who avoid registers with this search?"

"I know, but we just have to start somewhere. How many do we have left?"

"Only about six, I think, including your one from 2004. Those are good odds. Should we start looking for phone numbers?"

"Personally, Janey, I'm more interested in lunch first."

"Surprise, surprise. Soup and baguette?"

***

"What are you going to say to these people, 'hello, I'm looking for my long-lost brother who is a suspected murderer and I wondered if it might be you?'"

"I'll try to rephrase that, but you have a point, maybe I should note down how to begin the conversation. Should we look at Facebook and see what we find there?"

"Hmm, good idea." Rachael opened her phone and almost immediately came across an army private Donald Smith. "Look, Janey, he's the right age. Look at all the good wishes for his last birthday."

"And he's posted to Dreghorn just now. That's handy. It's just up the road."

"Shall we phone there too?"

"No. I don't think I want to phone anywhere. I'm going to pass our information to Mackay. He can run down the final investigation. I can't be seen to interfere with the enquiry."

"Wow. I hadn't thought of that." Rachael looked at Jane. She knew how much this search meant to her and also how much a guilty verdict against one of her brothers would take out of her. "Shall we have a walk and then see what we can find about Craig? Maybe your crazy stalker will join us."

"Nothing I'd like better right now."

The women had no company on their walk. There was no sight of the stalker or anybody else acting strangely. Jane was disappointed. She was tense and angry. Perhaps it would have made her feel better to confront her stalker and find out what he had in mind. On their way home, she suggested they take time to go into Drinkmonger, their favourite local wine shop, and pick up a decent bottle of wine for the evening.

***

Jane was standing at the kitchen sink filling the kettle for two mugs of chamomile tea after they got home. Rachael made a salad to go with their sliced, cold meat that would be their evening meal. Jane glanced out of the window and saw the thin, tattooed man staring up at their back window again. She didn't move, just asked Rachael to come and have a look at the guy.

"Those are some pretty grotesque tattoos, on his arms and

legs aren't they pet?" Rachael asked

"Yes, you can see them at the top of his chest too."

"Is that the man who followed you when you were running?"

"Yes, it's definitely the same guy," Jane said.

"He was in the Golf Tavern the other night when we were there with Tim."

"I didn't see him, but Tim mentioned him."

"You had your back to him in the pub."

"He was in the street when Tim and Bear picked me up to go for a run, too."

"I wonder what he wants."

"He wants a good kicking, that's what he wants, Rache. I am so sick of feeling like a target. Kicked off the murder enquiry and now stalked by a weirdo. Honestly, it all just sucks."

"Let's have something to eat, pet. Then we can delve into the Craig Smiths of Edinburgh this evening."

"Over a bottle of Sancerre."

"You talked me into it, Janey."

They dedicated their time to Craig Smiths and the delicate Sancerre in equal measure, they managed to reduce the large number of men to only eleven. Jane sent a text with the details to Angus and was surprised when he came back to her almost immediately.

"Will tell Mackay tomorrow. Met your brother, Troy. Nice guy. Take care."

Chapter Twenty-Five

When Tim and Bear called round to pick Jane up and go for a run the following morning, Rachael answered the door.

"What are you doing up at this time in the morning, Rache?" Bear asked.

"Somebody rang the doorbell. What are you doing here?"

"We came by to see if Jane was coming running with us today."

"Jane's already left."

"Well, she's not downstairs," Tim said.

"And neither is her stalker," Bear commented.

"He was in the back green again yesterday staring up at us while we were in the kitchen."

"Do you know where Jane was planning to go? I mean, was she waiting for us downstairs?"

"I don't know. She didn't say, just said she was going for a run and would see me when she got back." Rachael sounded a little anxious.

"Why don't you phone her, Rache? Then we can sort this out. It's probably just a misunderstanding."

Rachael ran through to the bedroom to get her phone and called Jane on speed dial. The phone rang in the living room. "Silly bitch hasn't taken her phone. Why didn't she take her phone?"

"I don't take my phone when I'm exercising," Tim said.

"Yes, but not being funny, you're six feet four and built like a brick shit house, Tim. Janey's not."

"I know, but I don't take it in case it gets broken, not because of my build."

"Sorry. I'm just worried."

"That's her personal one. Could she have taken her work

one by mistake?"

"The one she always left on silent? Probably."

"How long ago did she leave?" Bear asked.

"I don't know, I was half asleep. Let me think. Forty minutes ago, maybe. Certainly less than an hour."

"Have you any idea where she was going, what route she might take?"

"The only thing I can think of is that when we were looking up stuff on her brothers yesterday, we found a possible match for Donny, and he was in the army based at Dreghorn. She seemed curious about that and commented that she'd never visited an army barracks," Rachael said. "Do you think she's okay?"

"She probably is, but we'll just drive over to the barracks and see if we can track her down. Do you want to come with us, Rache?"

"No. No, Bear. Thanks. I'll call you if she comes home." Rachael watched the big men take the stairs two at a time and exit the stairwell from the apartment swiftly. "Where the fuck are you, Janey?" she said to herself.

***

It didn't take Tim long to drive from Bruntsfield to the Dreghorn Barracks. He pulled up to the side of the gates and asked the first soldier he saw if he had seen a woman out running this morning.

"Not exactly." He grinned. "There was a couple out. He was right skinny and lots of tattoos, I think I've seen him around here, but I'm new and just getting to know the lads. She was bonny but didn't seem that keen on joining him today. Some argument they were having."

"You didn't think to help her?" Tim asked.

"What and get involved in someone else's domestic? I don't think so, pal. I've got enough trouble with me own Mrs."

"What did they look like? Was he one of your lot?" Tim asked.

"I couldn't really see too well. He wasn't in uniform. She

looked quite fit. He was a tall skinny malinky long legs. No oil painting."

"And he had a lot of tattoos?"

"Look mate, I'm not being funny, but I took a quick look because of the racket and looked away. Didn't want to get involved."

Tim growled softly and smacked his right fist into his left hand.

"Which way did they go?" Bear asked.

"Down that way, I think." The soldier pointed down the street. "Heading towards the city bypass they were."

"Thanks. How long ago was this?" Bear got his question in before Tim had time to lose his temper with the squaddie. He wanted to keep the guy on side long enough to get the information they needed.

"Fifteen, maybe twenty minutes ago. If you listen hard enough, you can probably still hear her shouting at him. One bad tempered bitch, that one." He shook his head as he wandered back to what he should have been doing.

Bear bundled Tim back towards his car before he could say anything else to the man.

"Let's start looking. If we split up, we'll cover the area faster, so you go this way and I'll go that way. She can't be far. Come on, Tim, don't worry about what that squaddie said. Let's find Jane."

The men made their ways in opposite directions to try to pick up the trail Jane and the man might have left. His description made them think that it was probably her stalker. Neither of them could find any sign of Jane, but Tim found a hair scrunchy, similar to the type Jane wore and then further on he found a pen he had lent her that she had failed to return. Next, he found a wrist band that he recognised as belonging to Jane. It was dropped beside an old red car. Tim thumped the roof and was sure he a sound coming from the boot. He tried to open it, but it was locked.

"Jane, is that you?" Another creak came from within. "Once for yes and twice for no," he said. Tim listened carefully and was sure he heard one noise. "Don't worry, I'm here. I'm going to get you out."

He called Bear and told him where he was.

"I'll be right with you," Bear said.

Tim phoned the station for back up and said he thought they'd need a team of CSIs as well. Then he waited, talking softly all the time.

"The boot's locked," Tim said when Bear arrived.

"Is Jane inside?"

"Yes. I heard her. She responded to me when I called out to her."

"Right. Let's get her out. Jane, close your eyes and mouth. Tim, you stand back. I've got this," Bear said loudly and clearly. He took off his fleece and wrapped it around his hand, then he thumped the corner of the back window, the glass shuddered. He took out his phone. "Goodbye, old friend," he said. Then he pounded the glass window in the same place with his full force, and the corner of his phone. The phone cracked. A crazy pattern spread all across the window. Next, Bear thumped the centre of the window, and it finally gave way.

He stared at it, looking extremely satisfied. Then he worked at the panel behind the back seats until he raised it and revealed tools packed up in the boot.

"Your hearing's going, Timmy boy. No Jane in there."

"But are those hairs the same colour as hers? Those are long strands."

"Hey!" a guy called from across the street. "What the fuck are you doing with my uncle's car?"

"Oh no! Now the fun begins," whispered Tim.

***

Tim walked over to meet the man. "We are police detectives. I'm DC Myerscough, and this is DC Zewedu. One of our colleagues is missing and we're looking for her. I thought I heard sounds coming from the back of this car," he said.

"Probably the car groaning under the weight of his equipment."

110

"Who's your uncle then? Do you know why his car is parked on a double yellow line?"

"Does that justify bashing his window in?" The man glowered at Tim. "It's just so over the top. How dare you! Wait till I tell him."

"Don't be too hasty. We'll sort out compensation for your uncle, I promise you that. I'll personally buy him a brand-new car, any one he wants, but let's start at the beginning, shall we?"

"Wait just a minute, that's a big promise. You're only a detective constable. You can't make that kind of promise. You don't have the money."

"He really does," Bear whispered in the man's ear. "He'll be buying me a new phone too."

"Oh really. So, why's he a copper then."

"Long story. He wants to save the world," Bear said sarcastically.

"What's your name, anyway?" Tim walked with the man back to the front of the car. He saw PCs Scott Clark and Neil Larken pull up.

"What the hell's happened here?" Neil asked. He walked around to the back of the car and stared at the damaged window.

"Tim thought he heard Jane in the boot," Bear said.

"What? What's going on? Jane? Jane Renwick? Why would she be in the boot of a car?"

Tim explained what had happened throughout the morning and watched as the frown on Neil's face deepen.

"What the hell would she be thinking, coming all the way over here on her own if she's been stalked?"

"I've no idea what she was thinking or if she was thinking, but whatever, it wasn't a good idea."

"You don't say!" Bear said.

"What happened? Do you know?"

"She was meant to be coming for a run with Bear and me. But she'd left by the time we got to her flat. Rache said she decided to come for a run past the barracks to see what it was like because she'd found a soldier with her brother's name. He was based here. I suppose she wanted to see if she could see him."

"How would she recognise him?" Neil asked. I heard it's been a long time because her brother was a little boy last time she saw him."

"I thought about that," Tim said. "Even if the soldier here was her brother, what in heaven's name would make her think she'd recognise him as a grown man?"

"It's ridiculous when you put it like that, I know, and Jane's not usually silly or rash," Scott commented.

"And do you think her stalker took her?" Neil asked. He looked at the car. "It's looking pretty sad. You did that, Bear?"

They had forgotten about the man. Now he chimed in. "And *he's* going to buy my uncle a new car." He nodded towards Tim. "The other one says he can afford it."

"He can that," Neil said. "Do we know who the stalker is then?"

"A tall skinny guy with tattoos who goes running," Tim said.

"What's his name?" Neil asked.

Bear shook his head. "Sadly, that detail is missing as are any other clues to his identity and whereabouts. Believe me, I wish I knew."

"I wish I'd seen this coming," Tim said. "Where the hell is Jane now? Every minute that passes, I get more worried about her."

"Like to tell us what your uncle's name is?" Tim asked the man whose shoulder he was holding.

"Larry Cumming," the man said softly. "My uncle is Larry Cumming. Let me phone him."

"I'll check the number plate with the station, see if it matches to that name," Neil said.

The man walked a few paces away from the group and phoned his uncle on a rather old-looking mobile phone. Bear found himself envying it. He watched as the man stepped back towards the group.

"Uncle Larry's says he left his car outside his local garage with the key in the glove compartment so that it could get its

MOT yesterday, but the car was stolen. Both he and the garage reported it."

"That matches up with what I'm being told," Neil said.

"Uncle Larry asked if he could get his new car now because he doesn't want the old one in that state."

"I don't blame him. He couldn't have it back anyway. It's evidence."

"This isn't getting any better for him. Why do you need it? You bust it up by mistake. He'll need his tools."

"There'll be an investigation into our action," said Tim. "Tell him to go to this garage, Thomson's Top Cars and ask for Jamie Thomson. Tell your uncle to choose any car he wants and get Jamie to put it on my account."

"Really? That's sick, man. And his tools?"

"Give me his address and I'll drop them off by the end of the week, or I'll get him a new set. That sound okay?"

"I'll tell him. That's a real win for him."

"Can I get your name and address in case we need it?" Bear handed the man his notebook and he wrote out his details. He watched as the man wandered back across the road and continued walking towards the main road. He was whistling and walking much taller than when he first approached the two DCs.

"Now, you two get back to the station and you can report Jane's disappearance. We'll wait for the car to be towed," Neil said. "Wait till I tell Jane you think she sounds like a squeaky under carriage."

"I wish I could tell her now," Tim said quietly.

Chapter Twenty-Six

DI Regina Jallow called the room to order. There seemed to be more bacon rolls in the room than people. She couldn't help feeling the incident room was turning into more of a greasy spoon than a topflight crime-busting base. The noise level continued to rise. She slapped her folder on the desk in front of her and bellowed for silence. The irony was not lost on her.

Superintendent Miller and DCI Mackay walked in together as the volume reduced to a murmur.

"Too much going on to waste time," Miller said. "A witness saw DS Jane Renwick struggling with an attacker yesterday and she is now missing." He paused and looked around the room at the horrified faces in front of him.

"The witness didn't think to intervene?" Angus asked.

"Apparently not."

"Fucking hell. Is Jane all right?" Angus asked.

"What part of missing is unclear, McKenzie? Apparently, some fellow has been stalking her for several days. Local boys, Myerscough and Zewedu have seen him. They believe he is the kidnapper."

"Can they describe him?"

"The local team have sent a sketch artist over to meet with them. They've also put informal protection in place for her partner at the home she and Jane share until we get this enquiry concluded. Apparently, Myerscough and Zewedu are powerfully built and are friendly with the women. They appointed themselves as guardians."

"Tim Myerscough and Bear Zewedu," Angus nodded. "Nobody will get past that pair, and God help them if they try. Mind you, Rachael and Jane can be tough nuts too."

"I want to check if there is a connection between the recent murders in Edinburgh and this attack on DS Renwick," Miller said. "Check if DS Renwick or any of our other victims were involved in any cases heard by Lady Munro, Brian."

"Yes, sir."

"CSIs and the forensic teams are working to see if they can match the DNA with the traces we have. Jane dropped various items as she was being abducted and there were long strands of hair in the boot of a car where her trail stopped. Hopefully there will be traces of the kidnapper's DNA on those and the hairs will be found to be Jane's. Judy, can you chase those along?"

"Yes, sir."

"DS Renwick's wife told the local boys that she has also been spending her time tracing her family tree. She has reduced the list of people who might be her brothers from a large group to a small one. Angus, can you and Amar work on that?"

"Of course. Is all the information Jane and Rachael collected here? She only sent me a few details and said she'd email the rest to you, sir."

"Yes, her partner sent it to me. I'll print it off for you."

"That'll be useful, sir. Do we know if the brothers were adopted or changed their names?" Angus asked.

"No, McKenzie. That's something for you and Amar to find out.

"Thank you, sir," Amar said sarcastically.

"If there are no more questions, let's get busy," Miller said. "I want to reconvene at five o'clock and by then, I want answers.

***

It didn't take Judy long to find out that it would be at least the following day before she heard from the CSIs or forensics. After that she took an order for teas and coffees and distributed the drinks amongst the team.

"Brian," she said. "Do you need help checking out Lady Munro's cases?"

"Are you serious? That would be great. The woman only heard criminal cases recently and she certainly seemed to power through the work. I'm starting with the most recent and working backwards."

"Fine. Give me a bundle." She pulled up a chair to the side of his desk and they began to work their way through the cases.

"The family name was Smith, wasn't it?"

"Yes," said Amar. "But that doesn't really help because the only name in the cases is that of the accused, and we don't have that. You really have to read the wee bit underneath the title and that takes time."

"Yeh, I see what you mean. Come on then, I'll race you. Let's see what we can find." Judy picked up a sheet listing cases heard by Lady Munro in one hand, her tea in the other and began to read.

***

Amar and Angus divided up the work on the two brothers, Angus noticed that Amar was doing his fair share today. No shirking. He was pleased and felt it meant his new partner was beginning to accept him.

"I suppose that once we've worked out which ones are our persons of interest, we need to work out if they were in or near Edinburgh when all our four victims were killed."

"Yes, Amar, and the day Jane was kidnapped. It would make sense, but let's find our guys first."

"You take Craig, and I'll take Donny."

"No problem. I just wish we knew what the fuck had happened to Jane."

The two detectives studied the information available on the internet, and cross referenced it with the information they had about Jane's family.

"This one can't be him, his birthday's in January. See all the birthday wishes on Facebook," Angus said.

"When is our Donald Smith's birthday?"

"April."

"Look, I think I've found our Craig."

"Good. What do we know about him?"

"His birthday's September, he lives in Edinburgh, and he's one who's the right age. I'll Google him." Amar stopped talking briefly and then said, "Well, well, well, this one is a nurse. He would know about the human body well enough to kill someone with a sharp knife."

"How interesting, Amar. He would certainly know where to slice a victim to finish them off quickly. And look, it seems our Donald is in the army."

"A trained killer, then."

"It would seem so. But why would anyone attack this strange variety of victims?" Angus asked. "Let's speak to Brian and Judy and see what they've found."

***

Brian looked up as Angus and Amar walked over. "How's it going for you?" he asked.

"We think we've identified the brothers. Have you found a case that fits the bill?"

"There are three cases heard by Lady Munro that are recent where Jane was involved in the investigation and giving evidence," Brian said.

"The first is a wee girl who was abducted from a playground in Muirhouse, raped and strangled."

Judy's face showed the level of her disgust.

"But the killer was identified as her cousin, so it doesn't seem likely that a family member would seek revenge in that case."

"No, I see what you mean," Amar shook his head. "Ghastly crime, though."

"Yes. The next one is a child who was killed by a hit and run driver. The parents aren't married but live together and watched it happen. That doesn't fit either."

"What's the third one?" Angus asked.

"It seems even less likely. The wee girl was Aqua Hourston, but she died because of an accident at the dentist when she was having her teeth taken out. A young dentist miscalculated the amount of anaesthetic she should get."

"What a strange name. Parents shouldn't be allowed to make jokes when naming their children," Angus said.

"How bad would the dentist feel?" Judy asked.

"He calculated her weight in kilos instead of pounds. It really was an accident," Amar said. "Of course, he was charged with being responsible for her death."

"I doubt the family would see it as an accident. What was her father's name?" Brian asked.

"No idea. Single mother."

"Should we make arrangements to interview the families anyway?"

"Let's see what the boss thinks," Angus said.

Chapter Twenty-Seven

Jane woke up. She thought he must have put something into the tea he gave her. She was lying on a single bed. Clean sheet and the duvet looked new but had no cover. That really didn't matter. She didn't plan to be there long.

She sat up and looked around the room. No windows, but at least there was a light, a bare bulb dangling from the ceiling. He must have left it switched on. She saw the switch beside the door. One way in, one way out.

Jane rubbed her face. She felt disoriented and angry, but not afraid. She swung her legs over the side of the bed and stood up cautiously. Yes, her legs would carry her to the door. She walked across the room and tried the handle. It didn't budge. *That would have been too easy.* She thumped on the door.

"Help! Let me out! I'm a police detective. Let me out now!" She slapped the door. It shook but didn't give way. She rattled the door and shouted again. She kicked it but nothing gave way.

Jane turned and leant against the door. She gazed around the room. It was small. The bed was set against the wall opposite the door and there was a little chair beside the door with its back to the wall. There was a small table beside it and on it she noticed a sandwich and a bottle of water. It was only then that she realised she was hungry. Jane sat down on the chair and tore open the packet of sandwiches. Tuna mayonnaise. Not a favourite, but they would do. As she sat there, she noticed a bucket in the corner of the room. She guessed that this was to serve as her lavatory. Suddenly, she was overcome with misery. She sobbed. She put the sandwich down on the table, put her head in her hands and wept.

It was several minutes before she composed herself and fell

silent. *For goodness' sake, Jane, pull yourself together woman.* She picked up the sandwich and finished eating it, washing it down with the water. Then she sat and stared at the wall.

***

Jane must have nodded off because she had not heard the man come into the room. He was carrying a disposable plastic bag and was dressed entirely in black. He wore the same balaclava he had worn when he attacked her. Only his eyes were visible.

"That bag's not very pc, is it? Don't you care about the planet?" She wanted to get a response from him so that she might be able to identify him. "Why are you doing this to me?"

He didn't reply. He moved forward and picked up the wrapper from the sandwich. Jane lunged towards the door.

"Oh no you don't. You'll have to stay here for a while. Sorry I don't have a proper toilet for you, but you can use my shower to stay clean. This is just to keep you safe."

Jane was confused. His words did not sound at all threatening. If anything, they were caring, but his actions had robbed her of her freedom.

"This isn't a social visit. I don't want to stay long enough to use your shower. Why did you bring me here? I don't want to have to stay here to be safe. What do you want with me? Just let me go!" She screamed the last words.

Without saying another word, the man put the bag down on the floor in front of her and left the room. She crossed the room after him and tried to pull open the door before he could lock it, but he was too fast and too strong. She slapped the door with the palm of her hand and slid down until she was kneeling on the floor in front of it and sobbing.

***

After a while, Jane stopped crying. She was too tired to continue. She sat with her back to the door and began to think things through. She couldn't be sure that this man was her stalker, because she couldn't see him, but, on balance, she thought he probably was.

He must have followed her from the flat to the barracks. He could certainly move. What did he want with her? He hadn't hurt her, well apart from drugging her and kidnapping her. That was probably bad enough for one day. Why hadn't she just waited for Tim and Bear and talked them into going for a different run? Why had she been so damn mule-headed and gone off on her own? Where was she? How did the man get her here? So many questions and not one good answer.

She sighed and caught sight of the bag he had brought with him. She opened it up. A roll of toilet paper, a packet of wet wipes, this week's copy of *Take a Break* magazine with a pencil to allow her to do the puzzles, two bottles of water, a packet of ham sandwiches, an apple, and a small bar of chocolate.

Jane stared at the chocolate; it was exactly the same as the one the social worker had given her the day she was removed from her parents' home. What a coincidence.

Chapter Twenty-Eight

"Okay, Regina, let's hope the team have found something useful," Mackay said.

"Preferably Jane's whereabouts. Superintendent Miller wants to join the briefing. I've never seen him so worried."

Everybody in the room fell silent when Superintendent Miller walked in. The team stared at him with solemn faces. There were no jokes: nothing seemed funny. There was no chat. What was there to say? One of their own had gone missing and the only thing that mattered was to find her safe and well.

"I know the whole team has pulled together and is working extremely hard today. As you know, DS Jane Renwick has been abducted and her whereabouts are presently unknown. It would seem, however, that she has been the subject of a stalker recently and it may be that this is the man who has been involved in her disappearance," Miller said. He looked around the team.

"If I may, sir, perhaps Judy could tell us when we may expect to hear from forensics," Mackay said.

"I called, but it will be tomorrow at the earliest before they have anything for us, sir."

"Make sure it's tomorrow morning at the latest, Judy."

"Yes, sir."

"Brian, what did you find out about Lady Munro's recent caseload?" Mackay asked.

"Well, there was one case that stood out, sir. Lady Munro was the judge, and DS Renwick gave evidence."

"Are our other victims involved?"

"I don't know yet, sir, I'm waiting for a call back from the court, but they all seem to bugger off, I mean break for the day, about four o'clock. It'll probably be tomorrow before they get back to me."

"Is nobody but us treating this as a fucking emergency?" Miller exploded with rage. "One of our officers is missing. Don't they bloody care? McKenzie, Patel, tell us you have better news."

"I'm not sure, sir," Amar said.

"Just spit it out. You must have found something."

"From the information that Jane gathered and the stuff that came up on social media, we think we've found her brothers Donny and Craig."

"Good. Where are they and what do they do?"

"The one called Craig, Jane's younger brother, is a nurse in Crosshouse University Hospital in Kilmarnock. He lives in Edinburgh and commutes."

"He would know his way around a body well enough," Angus said. "The other one, Donald, Jane calls him Donny, is in the army."

"So, he's trained to kill," Amar added.

"Not necessarily, he could be a musician," Mackay said.

"Not according to his social media, he's not."

"Surely members of the military aren't allowed a social media presence," Regina said.

"Maybe not all of them, but this one has."

"What about tattoos? Jane's stalker is said to have a lot of tattoos."

"Yep, they both seem to have tattoos," Amar said. "And I found this case that Lady Munro heard where Jane was involved too. A wee girl died as a result of a mistake made by a young dentist. But it was a one parent family, and the father wasn't on the birth certificate."

"What happened?" Regina asked.

"The child died, apparently because the dentist who was removing her teeth calculated her weight in kilos instead of pounds and so she got too much anaesthetic," Angus explained.

"I see, are any of our other victims involved?"

"We don't know yet, boss. The courts seem to close up early and it will probably be tomorrow before we hear anything."

"The dentist was young and inexperienced and there was no intention to harm the child, so he wasn't found guilty of murder, but of a lesser crime, what do they call it, Angus?" Amar asked.

"Culpable homicide."

"That sounds worse," Judy muttered.

"He only got sentenced to a few years in jail, five years nine months, not life," Angus said.

"He'll be out in less than three years with good behaviour," Amar said. "Of course, his career as a dentist is over."

"I suppose not too many people would trust him going forward," Jallow said.

"Boss, we wondered if we should go and speak to the family of the child?" Angus asked.

"Not at this stage. I'd rather we found out more about the whole case and whether all our victims were involved in it before we go invading the misery of that family. Brian, I want you working on that," Mackay said. "It might be a good idea to catch up with the brothers, though. The nurse is in Crosshouse, that's not too far. You and Judy go there and sound him out, Amar. Where is the army guy based, Angus?"

"Dreghorn barracks in Edinburgh, sir."

"Fine. You visit him there with one of the local lads. I want this all cleared up and DS Renwick back in action with us as soon as. Do I make myself clear?"

"Yes, sir."

Chapter Twenty-Nine

Rachael opened the door to find Tim and Bear looking anxious.

"Have they found her?"

"No, not yet, but it's just a matter of time until they do. In the meantime, we'll make sure one of us is always here with you to keep you safe," Tim said.

"Isn't that a bit like shutting the stable door when the horse has bolted? I'm perfectly capable of looking after myself." Rachael sighed. "Jane has already been abducted and nobody is interested in me. You are both quite surplus to requirements." The men followed her into the flat and headed for the kitchen where Rachael put on the kettle.

Bear stood looking out of the window. "Isn't that guy looking up at your flat the same one who watched Jane when she came running with us?

"Oh God, yes. Why is he still hanging around if he's got her?"

"Maybe he doesn't. Maybe he does and he still wants you," Tim said. "Are you taking the first shift, Bear?"

"No problem, Tim. Mel's at work anyway."

"Thanks. Gillian is still a mess after Zelay's death. It might be better if I were with her tonight."

"I can't see either of your lovely ladies being thrilled at you spending so much time here. And what does the boss say?"

"The girls are incredibly supportive, and Hunter has given us all time off we need to make sure you're safe. Believe me, Rachael, this is a done deal," Tim said.

"I don't remember agreeing to it."

"Nobody asked you."

Chapter Thirty

I told myself that I wouldn't come to another one of these, but it is so hard to keep away. The journalists' chatter is almost more fun than the police statement. I managed to avoid the chatty girl this time but found myself beside the suspicious man who kept asking questions and didn't stop today.

"Hey! Here you are again. This seat free?"

I nodded and looked away, hoping he would just shut up, but no such luck.

"Did you hear that judge's home wasn't broken into. She must have known her killer, I suppose. I heard she was signed up to a dating site too. You never know who you're going to meet there, do you?"

"No. Isn't that the point? You meet someone new."

"Aye. True enough. Which paper did you say you worked for again? Look here they come."

Thank goodness they started more promptly than usual. I didn't have to answer his nosy question. The police still have no idea that it's me. Well, why would they? I wish they hadn't found my DNA at some of the scenes. I suppose I could just say I was visiting, but I got my hand covered in the man's blood. That's awkward. What are the chances they'd have one of my fucking brothers on the force? What shitty luck! I shouldn't have been so careless, but I never thought about it. I just want justice for the wee one. The system failed her so I'm making sure I sort that for her, and the pigs don't know anything. Nothing. Nada. Simple as.

Suddenly, I notice I've stopped listening. They were saying that there had been significant developments. One of their officers has been abducted and they believe it is the next move by the murderer. They can't give us a photo of them because it might upset the investigations. They will update us as soon as they can. What a lot of bloody nonsense. Abduction? Where would I abduct him to? I don't want to be funny, but why would I?

If it wasn't me, who was it? And which officer is it? They wouldn't say. My nosy friend asked the question I wanted to.

"Superintendent Miller, if you think there's a connection between the murders and the abduction of your officer, is it the same officer who has a family connection with the killer?"

"I can't comment on that right now. You understand. The search for our officer must be the priority."

"But not over catching the killer," the nosy one said.

"Our thoughts are the perpetrator is one and the same."

"But you don't know that, so surely the search for the murderer can't be diverted."

I noticed that the cops looked angry. After a few moments, the woman cop spoke. "Believe me, Paul. You are Paul Jones from The Scotsman, aren't you?"

"That's me."

"Well, believe me when I say there are enough dedicated officers in Scotland to make sure that both investigations are fully pursued."

"What do you want us to print, DI Jallow?" the chatty girl from before said. "Perhaps our readers can help."

"We are looking for a tall, thin man with heavily tattooed limbs and chest who may be able to help with our enquiries. He is known to go running in the Links and across the Meadows in Edinburgh. If any of your readers may be able to help us trace this man, they should phone the help line or Crimestoppers."

"Can I quote you on that, DI Jallow?"

"Please do," she said.

"Is there a mock-up or photofit of what this man looks like?" the nosy man asked.

"We don't have a detailed enough description to provide that, I'm afraid. Just a general description," the superintendent said.

"But it is quite a distinctive description," DI Jallow added.

"That's disappointing, but we'll print the description and see if you get a response," the chatty girl said.

"Oh, we always get a response." DI Jallow grimaced. "We get confessions from those who tell us they committed the crime we are investigating, others who claim they killed the dinosaurs and yet more who have never liked their great uncle Toby and believe he is the man we are looking for."

Everybody laughed. "If you discover who killed the dinosaurs that could be ground-breaking news," the chatty girl said. "Keep us up to date on that."

"All right everybody, let's call it a day. Thank you for your attendance." The superintendent gathered up his papers.

I saw him whispering to DI Jallow as they left the room. I thought I saw him looking directly at me. He waved and I got nervous. Did they know I wasn't a journalist? Were they going to call me out? Fuck. What had I done to draw attention to myself? I felt myself going red. I felt my temperature rise and my breath became short and laboured. My palms were sweaty. I noticed my pen felt sticky. I was in the middle of the row, and I couldn't run.

Thank God. The nosy guy next to me whispered in my ear. "Did you see that? The superintendent signalled to me. I wonder if I'm going to get extra info. Look, sorry, but I'm off to see what that nod meant. Wish me luck. I hope it's a juicy tidbit."

I watched him shove his way to the front of the room and chase after the cops, but the door swung shut behind them before he got there. I watched a tall red-haired detective stood and barred the way. I couldn't help smiling. It seemed my nosy companion was wrong, there was no extra information just for him.

My heart returned to a normal beat, but my armpits were sweaty. I noticed my grip on my notebook was tight. My knuckles were white with the tension. Gradually, I released my grip and popped my notebook and pen into my pocket. I followed a group out into the foyer.

I didn't want to become embroiled in conversation so I left as quickly as I could and headed for home. My home that didn't have an abducted detective under the bed, or anywhere else for that matter. I wonder who did that? Or could it be a hoax the cops had put out? Curiouser and curiouser.

Chapter Thirty-One

"My goodness, it's a long time since I was in Crosshouse Hospital," Judy said.

"I've never been here. When were you here?" Amar asked.

"My dad had cancer and he got his chemotherapy here. I used to bring him."

"That's heavy. How is he, now?" Amar asked.

"He's doing okay, thanks. But those were long sessions, you can imagine."

"It would have been. It's always worse watching someone else you care about going through something like that yourself."

"That's true. But there was an upside. The hospital gave us both lunches. We came on Tuesdays and that was leek and potato soup day. We got a sandwich too."

"Sounds okay. I could do with that today. God, what is the parking like?"

"Lots of people park here for free and then take the bus into Kilmarnock for work. Parking is always horrendous."

"Are we going to get a space? We may have to park in the village and walk back."

"Fuck that," Judy said. "Look, look, there's a space. Quick, get it!"

"Thank the Lord. We're still ages away from the entry. Should we leave breadcrumbs so we can find our way back to the car?" Amar smiled. "Come on, let's get a move on. We'll be late."

***

Amar and Judy walked up to the main entrance. Several

patients were outside sitting in the sun underneath the 'No Smoking' signs puffing on cigarettes and sucking on vapes. The detectives glanced at each other, ignored the offenders, and made their way to the reception desk.

"Detective constables Patel and Marsh," Amar said, showing his identification. "We're hoping to speak to one of your nurses, Craig Smith."

"I phoned ahead and was told he is working in your stroke ward 4d today," Judy said.

"Let me have a look for you," the receptionist said. He's not in any trouble, is he?"

"It's not that, but he may be able to help us with an ongoing investigation," Judy said.

"Oh, that's alright then, he's such a nice person. Yes. He's in. If you follow the signs to 4d you'll find him there. Along to the left and follow the signs to the ward."

"Thanks," Amar said. He turned and led the way along the corridor.

"There's even a shop," Judy said. "I might go in and buy a bar of chocolate."

"Let's get on with this. You can get the chocolate on the way out."

Amar and Judy marched in step to the ward. There was an extremely young student nurse sitting at the desk.

"Can I help you?" she asked.

Amar showed his identification and asked if they could speak to nurse Craig Smith. He watched as the girl turned around. She shouted to a man walking towards them.

"Is Craig still in with Mrs Davies?"

"No, I think he's taking his break. Do you want me to get him?"

"Yes please. These coppers want to speak to him."

"What's he done?" he asked.

"We hope he may be able to help us with an ongoing enquiry," Judy said. She saw a tall thin man walking towards them carrying a mug. He wore a turban and had his beard neatly plaited.

"Craig, these are police looking to speak to you," the

student nurse said.

"No problem," he said in a broad Glasgow accent. He turned to the girl. "Is the family room free?"

"Yep."

"Follow me. We'll get a bit of privacy in here."

"Excuse me for asking, but are you nurse Craig Smith?"

"Yes, that's me." He sat on one chair and indicated that Judy and Amar should sit too. "You're now going to tell me that I'm not exactly who you had expected to see."

"No, not exactly," Amar said. "Did you change your name at some point?"

The man laughed. "No, my father was a Scottish soldier. He met my mother when he was on a tour of duty in India. He's not really religious, which Mum is, so I got her religion, but Dad wanted me named for his grandfather, so I got Grandpa Smith's name. He named my brother after my uncle, so he's Gordon. Anyway, enough of my family history, how may I be of assistance to you today?"

"I'm not at all sure that you can, Mr Smith, but let's see," Amar said. "What is your full name?"

"Craig Smith."

"What's your date of birth?"

The man replied and Amar looked at Judy. He nodded.

"Were you adopted, or were you ever taken from your parents to live in care?"

"No! What is all this about?"

"How many siblings do you have, sir?"

"I told you, one brother. I can phone him if you want to speak to him."

"That won't be necessary, Mr Smith," Judy said. "When was the last time you were in Edinburgh?"

"I always take a week during the festival and go to a few shows. I usually stay with my brother. Again, you are welcome to check that with him."

"So, you haven't been to Edinburgh since last August?" Amar clarified.

"No, I haven't."

"And you don't have a sister at all?" Judy asked.

131

"Or a half-sister, perhaps?"

"No!" Craig said. "You know, I'm really an extremely patient man, but this intrusion is now bordering on offensive and I'm almost at the end of my rope. If you won't tell me what this is about and you have no further questions for me, I will get back to work."

"Yes, of course. Thank you for your time, Mr Smith. We won't detain you any further," Judy said. She and Amar stood up and followed Craig Smith out of the little room.

***

Back in the car, Amar looked at Judy. "That was awkward," he said.

"That's the understatement of the day. As soon as I saw him, I knew it couldn't be the right guy."

"Yeh, me too, Judy. But if we hadn't asked him the questions to completely rule him out, Jallow and Mackay would have had us for breakfast."

"Would they, though? I mean, really?"

"Yes, I know, but we'd have got a roasting for not making sure he was the wrong man. So, we have the wrong Craig Smith. What do we do now?"

"Head back to base and search for another man with the same man and the same date of birth as our nurse."

"I can't blame him for getting grumpy, Judy. Our questions must have sounded really idiotic because we didn't tell him why we were asking them before he sent us packing."

"Damn! I forgot to get my chocolate. I don't suppose you want to make a detour on the way back?"

Amar shook his head.

"Thought not."

***

"He was wearing what?" Mackay shouted.

"A turban, sir. The man is a Sikh. His mother is an Indian national and his father was serving in the British Army. That's

132

how they met, sir," Amar replied.

"So, we have the wrong man."

"Yes sir. There is no way that this nurse is our killer," Amar said. "Apart from anything else, he is closer to my skin colour than Jane Renwick's. It was obvious as soon as we met him that he wasn't Jane's brother, but we asked him questions just to eliminate him completely from enquiries."

"As far as I can see that means you have more work to do to find a man with the same name and the same date of birth as the man you met today."

"Yes, DI Jallow."

"Well, what are you waiting for? Off you go. And try not find another wrong man."

"Yes, boss," Amar and Judy said quietly.

As they left the room, Jallow looked at Mackay and shook her head. "Who would have bloody believed it? I don't know about you, sir, but I need an extraordinarily strong coffee, can I get you one?"

"I need something a great deal stronger than that, but yes, a coffee would be a good start."

Chapter Thirty-Two

Tim sat opposite Rachael at the breakfast bar. He looked at his friend and took a sip of his beer.

"How did you and Bear get on today?"

"Fine. We played *Monopoly*. He does hate to lose."

They were waiting for the pizza Tim had ordered. Neither he nor Rachael felt like cooking, but he knew he should make sure she ate something. Pizza was all he could get her to agree to.

"Where the hell is she, Tim?"

"If I knew that she'd be here, and we'd need an extra pizza."

"How does she do that eating like a horse thing and stay so slim?"

"My guess is her running has a lot to do with it."

"Why couldn't she have been in the boot of that car? Bear said you offered to buy the owner a new car, anything he liked. Is that true?"

"Sort of," Tim said. "I gave him Jamie Thomson's card for Thomson's Top Cars and told him to take his pick from the forecourt. Those are all the second-hand cars. I admit I did phone Jamie and asked him not to let the man rip me off. I'm not keen to buy him a high-end Volvo to replace his aged Citroen."

Rachael laughed. "Like you would have noticed the difference in *your* bank balance."

"I know, but nobody likes to pay more than they have to, not even me."

"I suppose that's true. How's Gillian, by the way? I know she was devastated by Zelay's murder. How long had they worked together?"

"She'd only known him a couple of years, but she has always thought very highly of him and made a point of keeping up with what he was doing and publishing, even before she knew him."

"So, she knew of him before she worked with him?"

"Yes. Always held him in high regard. I just wish she would stop crying. I can't do anything for her and can't seem to be of any comfort to her. I had planned that we'd go away on a good holiday, maybe Goa or The Maldives, but even that's not taking her mind off things."

"When Jane gets back, I think we should take a holiday."

"She'll probably want to go to Paris and wander around The Louvre every day, or to Florence, and spend all the time in The Uffizi. You'd be bored stiff," Tim said.

"No, I wouldn't. I'd be with Jane and hold her hand and never let her go."

"Except when she was running."

"Except when she was running," Rachael agreed.

The doorbell rang. "Pizza," they said in unison, and Tim went to the door.

"I'm sure I'm not in any danger from collecting pizza from my own front door, Tim. Really."

"Well, right now I'm not sure, so if it's all the same to you, I want to get it."

"We don't agree on that but bring it through to the living room. Let's go and eat pizza."

"You talked me into it. Do you have another beer?"

"Help yourself from the fridge. Will you bring one through for me too?"

"Of course."

Tim wandered back through from the kitchen to the living room with two opened bottles of beer. "Did you just get me to bring the beers so that you could start the pizza without me? I bet you took the biggest slice."

Rachael smiled at him and held out her hand for her beer.

"I suppose it's not all that surprising that Gillian is so badly affected because she had met that judge that was killed too."

"Oh really, Lady Munro? When did your girlfriend start

mixing in such grand circles?"

"It's not like that. She was on a jury in a horrible case that Lady Munro heard. I remember Gillian was terribly upset by it."

"What was it about?"

"I can't remember exactly. She wasn't able to say very much." Tim paused. "Do you want that last slice of pizza?"

"Go ahead. I've had plenty." Rachael finished her beer. "I understand Lady Munro only really hears fairly heavy criminal cases now."

"Yes, the one Gillian was involved in was about the death of a wee girl. Very sad, especially when a child died."

"It is. I would like to have a baby."

"Me too."

"But not together." Rachael laughed.

"Probably not." Tim smiled. "Shall we have another beer, or shall we call it a night?"

"I think we should call it a night. Are you okay in the spare room?"

"Absolutely."

"If you need anything, just help yourself, Tim. And if you can't find something, give me a shout."

Chapter Thirty-Three

"Who are you? What have I done to you that warrants you keeping me here?"

Jane looked at her captor but, as usual, he didn't reply. She couldn't tell what he looked like because of that damn balaclava and the black clothes. All she could see was his eyes. They did not look unkind or crazed as she had expected. They just looked weary and sad.

"I'll need some clean clothes. I've been wearing these for ever and I stink. You said I could use your shower." She sat on the bed and stared up at him. "So, can I?"

He nodded and signalled that she should stand up and walk in front of him. Jane tried to get her bearings, but he took her from the box room into an enclosed hall and indicated that she should go into the room on her left. It was a small internal shower room that contained a shower stall, a toilet, and a small sink.

"You hand me out your clothes, I'll wash and dry them while you're in the shower."

"How long do you think it takes me to have a shower?"

He shrugged. "Take it or leave it."

Jane peeled off her dirty clothes and opened the door a fraction to hand them out. It was then she noticed that there was no mirror in the room. That was probably a good thing, she doubted she looked too good. She saw the white towel hanging on the hook at the back of the door and that there was no lock. Just then she heard a click as a lock on the other side of the door was rammed home. She shook her head. This was not what she had hoped for, but at least she could use the toilet as well as take a shower.

Looking around, she noticed a bottle of body wash but no

shampoo. Not a problem, it would do, she had washed her hair in worse. She remembered the month she had spent as a teenager, crossing America on a Greyhound bus, and smiled. Crossing the salt flats of Utah at dawn when the sun shone pink across the plateau was a sight she would never forget, nor the first time she'd seen the Golden Gate Bridge.

She remembered how she had often taken an overnight bus to avoid having to pay for a room. A bowl of soup and as many of the free crackers as she could carry made a meal. She had also used the small toilet cubicle in the back of the bus for a quick wash and even washed her hair with the hard little bars of soap left for the passengers.

Old ladies on the buses would tut and look at her disapprovingly while students on their own adventures would smile and nod. Then she would watch as they followed her example. What an exciting month it had been. Then she had joined the police.

That was exciting too. This experience was anything but. However, body wash cleaned her hair as well as her body.

When she was clean and dry, she wrapped the towel around herself and tucked the opening tightly under her arm. The man had shown no inclination towards impropriety, but she didn't want to go looking for trouble. She tried the door on the off chance that it would open, but no such luck. Maybe he would let her go if she offered it to him. No, the idea was too revolting.

She had no idea how much time had passed until there was a knock on the door.

"Yes," she said.

The door opened and he handed back her clothes.

"Knock when you're dressed," he said. When she did, he unlocked the door and motioned for her to walk back to her room, her prison, in front of him.

As soon as she was inside, he locked the door behind her.

Jane noticed a smell of disinfectant and realised that he had emptied and cleaned her bucket. Then she saw a plastic carrier bag and went over to open it. Her only excitement was to inspect the contents of the plastic bags he left. Today there was a copy of 'Chat' magazine, packet of cheese sandwiches, a banana and a bag of cheese and onion crisps. Nothing to drink. Then she noticed the flask and bottle of water under the chair. More excitement: what was in the flask? *Builders' tea. Oh well, it'll make a change from water, and it'll be warm.*

She flicked through the magazine and then lay down on the bed and wept. *What could she possibly have done that was so bad that this man wanted to hold her prisoner?* She missed Rachael, she missed her home, she missed her job, she missed her freedom.

Were they even looking for her? Of course, they were. Would they know where to look? She had no idea where she was or why she was here. How could they possibly find her? He had taken her phone. Oh, for goodness' sake, self-pity wouldn't help. She was an experienced police detective and just needed to make a plan to get away the next time he came in. She sniffed to clear her nose and picked up the sandwiches, she opened the packet and began to stare at the different parts of the room and the furniture at her disposal to think seriously about how she was going to overcome her captor and make her escape.

She wrinkled up her nose. This cheese was tasteless. She ate it all, even the crusts. She needed her strength. What she would give for a tasty slice of stilton from *Ian Mellor's Cheesemonger* on a piece of fresh French bread.

Chapter Thirty-Four

Jallow walked over to Angus. "McKenzie, are you going over to Edinburgh tonight?"

"Eventually, boss. I live there."

"Not so much of the smart mouth, okay?"

"Okay. What do you need?"

"Jane's older brother, Donald, it seems he's a squaddie posted to Dreghorn Barracks just now. Could you grab one of the locals and go over to see if you can speak to him tomorrow morning?"

"Yes boss. But don't you want me to go with Amar?"

"Not really. After the fiasco with the brother, or not brother, Craig, I'd rather not spend too much of our time on this. As you'll be in the city anyway, go and see what you can find out tomorrow and then come back over and we'll hear what you learned."

"No problem, boss. Consider it done."

***

Rachael's doorbell rang early the following morning. "Tim, that'll be Bear," she said as she went to open the door. "Oh, Angus. Hello. What are you doing here?"

"Nice to see you too, DC Anderson."

"Sorry. I didn't mean it like that. Have you got news about Jane?"

"No, sadly not, Rache. Greater minds than mine are working on that. I was told by Neil at the station I might find Tim with you."

"Yes, he's here and just about to grab a coffee. Do you want one?"

"Please."

The doorbell rang again. "Goodness, it's like Waverley Station here this morning," Rachael said.

"Don't worry, I'll get my own coffee," Angus called back.

"Bear, come on in. I suppose you want a coffee too."

"Yes please, Rache. I wouldn't mind something to eat as well. Tim, Angus, hello. Have you opened a coffee shop, Rache?"

"Don't be cheeky."

"Bear, can Angus and I leave you to negotiate your breakfast with Rachael? We're off to see if we can find Jane's soldier brother."

"Why are you going?" Rachael asked. "Isn't it an MIT thing?"

"Generally, yes. But a couple of my MIT colleagues were sent to interview the younger brother and spent a large part of their afternoon chatting to a Sikh gentleman who was not adopted and has no sisters."

"Oh, God."

"Exactly, Rache. So, my DI asked me to stop by Dreghorn Barracks with a local guy and speak to the soldier brother because I am in Edinburgh anyway and it'll take least of our time. I thought I'd stop by here and pick-up Tim or Bear as my 'local guy'. I want to get there early so there is less chance of missing the brother."

"I'm handing over to Bear here, so I can come with you, Angus." Tim drained his coffee mug and stood up.

"Can't I come too?" Rachael asked.

"I don't think that would be a good idea. You know the boss has told you to take time off while Jane is missing."

"I know all that, but I'm getting stir crazy here and the longer Jane is out there without us finding her the more likely she is to turn up dead. I really couldn't bear it. I'm so scared for her."

Bear put his arm around her. "Come on, none of that. You need to be strong for Jane. Why don't we go out for a walk and stop for coffee, and I'll get my breakfast? No offence, but this muesli and croissants rubbish you have here is really not to my taste. I need proper food."

"I'm so sorry. I'll punish my personal breakfast shopper

severely. Anyway, a walk might help. I'll go and get a jacket then."

"Right, we're off. If you two go out, make sure you keep her safe, Bear."

"For the love of God, don't teach your Granny to suck eggs, Tim. I'll make sure Rache is fine."

Bear winked at Tim, poured himself a coffee, sat at the breakfast bar, and waited for Rachael to return. He watched as Tim and Angus left the flat. Then he wandered about the kitchen and gazed out of the window. There was a man staring up at the back of the block of flats. He was slim and dressed in black. Bear couldn't tell whether the man was looking at Jane and Rachael's flat or just at the building in general. Bear thought he looked like the man Jane had spoken about with Tim and himself; the man who had stalked her.

Suddenly their eyes met. Bear then had no doubt that the man was staring at this flat, he was looking straight at Bear.

"Shall we go?" Rachael asked.

"Perhaps I haven't given muesli enough of a chance."

"Pull the other one, big man. Let's go and get you something you like to eat. I'm sure we can find a greasy spoon that will serve you a bacon roll."

Bear looked back out of the window. The man was gone.

"There was that guy looking up at your flat again. Do you want me to call for back up?"

"No. I don't want any more fuss. If he's there he can't be the one who has Jane, can he? He's just a weirdo."

"Have you or Jane worked out what he's after?" Bear asked.

"In case you hadn't noticed, Jane is missing. Is nobody else even bothered about that? She might be dead by now."

"Of course. We're all worried about her. You and I both know that Jane is much too stubborn just roll over and die. After all, she is an experienced police detective." Bear tried to cheer her up. "Come on then, a greasy spoon is calling."

They trotted down the stairs and Bear moved to open the door, and, putting his good manners aside, he left the close first, with his body protecting Rachael, and he was surprised to find the same man directly in front of him. Bear swept his left arm around Rachael and shoved her across the road and out of danger. His right arm provided a barrier between her and the man.

"Look out, Bear. A knife!"

Just as Bear turned away, he saw the flash of a metal blade in the man's hand. Bear grabbed the man's wrist, but he transferred the knife to his other hand and Bear felt the blade slash through his sleeve and cut his forearm.

"Shit," said Bear. He held his arm.

"You fucking bastard," Rachael shouted. She turned around and grabbed the man. "Where's Jane?" she said through clenched teeth. She couldn't hold him. He was just too strong. He wriggled free and dropped his knife and ran towards Bruntsfield Links.

"Let's get back up to the flat. Will you need to go to hospital?"

"I doubt it's that deep."

"Okay, Doctor Zewedu. But I'll clean your wound and bandage it for you."

"Bring the knife, will you? We can check if it's the same one that was used in the murders."

"Oh God. Do you think Jane is dead?"

"No. But my arm is damn sore."

Rachael took a clean, paper tissue out of her pocket and lifted the knife off the ground. "I hope there's good DNA on that."

"I doubt it. He was wearing gloves, but it might be the same knife. You know, I've had about enough of this investigation. So far, my friend's been kidnapped, I've ruined my phone and had my arm sliced open."

"Poor Bear. If we're not going out for breakfast, I don't have bacon, but I could scramble you some eggs and I have cold ham. Would that work for you?"

"Did I tell you I love you?"

"Don't start that. You only love a cooked breakfast. I'm spoken for and so are you. How is Mel? God, I'll need to phone her and tell her what's happened. Honestly, when are you going to propose to that long suffering woman?"

"After my arm stops hurting. I hope my good lady is working

hard today. One of us should be and it might as well be her. I don't suppose we could get more coffee to go with the ham and eggs?"

"Right after I've seen to that cut."

***

It didn't take Angus and Tim long to get to Dreghorn Barracks. The soldier who greeted them knew Tim from the few days previously when he and Bear had been looking for Jane.

"Did you find that woman you were after?" he asked.

"Haven't caught up with her yet," Tim said. He didn't want to give the man any extra information that might reflect on Jane's situation and that the squaddie could leak to the press. "We're looking for one of your lads today, Donald Smith. Is he around?"

"Donny? Should be, I think. Let me call over and find out where he's working. I won't be a moment."

He picked up a black phone and Angus heard him ask for Donny Smith. The man frowned as he listened to the reply. He didn't speak. He looked slightly puzzled and then hung up. He turned back to Angus and Tim.

"I'm sorry, gents. He's on leave."

"Where's he gone?" Angus asked.

"When's he back?" Tim asked.

"None of my business on both counts."

"Does he have friends that he might have told where he was going?" Tim asked.

"I have no idea."

"Look, mate, we're hoping he might be able to help us. It's important. Have you any idea where he might be? We really need to talk to him." Angus looked at the guy and hoped he might be able to give them something, anything that might lead them to Donny Smith and hopefully even their murderer.

"I honestly don't know where he is. He's got a wee flat down Fountainbridge way, but he rents that out. I doubt he'll be there, but if there's a new tenant going in, he might have taken time to sort the place out. Otherwise, who would bother to go on leave

144

to Fountainbridge from here?"

"I don't suppose you know where in Fountainbridge?" Tim said.

"Well, you'd be right there, and I care less. So, if it's all the same to you, I'm going to get back to work before I get a bollocking."

Angus and Tim turned to go and then they heard the man shout.

"Robbie, you know where Donny's off on leave?"

"Couple of weeks at home. He's doing it up a bit between tenants."

"Where's his flat again?"

"Dundee Street. Can't remember the number."

"Hope that helps," the squaddie shouted to them.

Angus waved his thanks and then turned to Tim and said, "It would be one of the longest streets, wouldn't it?"

"Let's check the property register. I don't fancy having to walk up and down all those stairs looking for D. Smith."

"Well said that man." Angus smiled. They drove back to the station at Fettes where Tim was based and where, until recently, Angus had worked too. As Angus navigated the Edinburgh one-way traffic system, Tim looked at his phone.

"I missed a call from Rachael. I'll just call her back."

"Rache? You were looking for me."

"What? Fuck, no. Did you manage to hold him? No don't worry." Tim glanced at Angus. He took the phone away from his mouth and said, "Bear's been slashed by Jane's stalker." He spoke to Rachael again. "How bad is it? Do you need us to swing back and take the big man to hospital?"

Angus looked at him anxiously.

Tim shook his head. "Okay, if you're sure. Yes, we'll come back and take him and the knife to the mortuary so that Meera can check if the same knife was used.

"But Rache, stay where you are and keep the door locked. Angus and I've got a lead for Donny, but it might take a while to make it good. Tell Bear to come down and wait at the foot of your stair. We won't be long. Keep in touch. We'll let you know as soon as we find Donny."

Chapter Thirty-Five

I appreciated the thought of the magazine with the puzzles, but it didn't keep me busy for more than an hour. I can't tell if it's day or night because there's no window and that bucket stinks.

I try to exercise. I mean I do exercise, but the room is small, so I jog on the spot, do sit ups, squats and lunges. I need to keep fit. Then I sit on the chair and try to work out a way to take him by surprise and escape. There's nowhere to hide so I need to be fast.

In the middle of my daydreams the door unlocks. He says nothing, just hands in another bag. He doesn't ever say very much, and he's never hurt me, but he makes sure I can't see him, can't identify him. Why am I here? Why me? I really don't understand.

Oh no, an egg mayo sandwich. Does anybody like those or do they just make them to use leftover bread and mayo? There's water, an apple and right in the corner of the bag another of those same little bars of chocolate.

It makes me think of the last time I saw Donny and Craig. We were only children. Hiding under the bed when the doorbell rang. We always did. It was one of Dad's house rules. There weren't many: don't answer the door, hide under the bed if the bell rings, one portion of chips is plenty. There may have been more, but those are the ones I remember.

I didn't even know if my brothers were still alive until all these murders started. It's horrible to think that someone closely related to me could do such wicked things. I remember trying to keep up with Donny when I was wee. It drove him mad, but he always tried to protect me and Craig from our folks' tempers when they couldn't get their fix. But he couldn't protect me from Dad's lust. Only Mum could have done that,

146

but she was usually off her face and couldn't have cared less.

My memories of Craig aren't so clear, but he was younger. I remember him wailing a lot. Who could blame him? He often had a soggy bottom, and he was always hungry. So were Donny and I, but at least we could go on the rob. I can't tell you the number of nets of Babybels, packets of cold meat, bars of chocolate and pints of milk we took. Packets of nappies were a problem, they were too bulky, so we became adept at taking two or three out of a packet quickly and putting the pack to the back of the shelf. We never stole crisps because the bags made too much noise.

Of course, we never walked out empty-handed. We always bought something small like a carton of juice, near-date fruit, or a packet of candy. It was usually something to eat or drink we'd get with money found on the ground, left in phone boxes, or begged from passers-by, but sometimes we'd pick a broken pack of nappies that only cost a few pence. We'd always giggle outside the shop about how a packet of nappies could have some missing and then run home to Craig with our stolen treasures.

I remember how his little face would light up when we had chocolate or candies. Donny and I had to keep him quiet, though. If Mum or Dad had found our stash, we'd have lost it. They always had the munchies because of the amount of hash they smoked. Now I think back, they really were fucking awful parents.

I turned my face to the wall and began to cry. I wondered about the baby in Mum's belly when we were taken. Was it a boy or a girl? Maybe I had a sister. Had the kid even made it? Did the social worker remember to come and save them? Oh God I hoped so. Those wasters didn't deserve to be parents not that they were any kind of parents to us anyway. They fucked, and were fertile, and that was our bad luck.

No, I couldn't wish never to have lived. I would never have seen the beautiful art in the world, wouldn't be able to do a job I enjoy but most of all, I wouldn't have known the love I have with Rachael.

I have to keep up my spirits and keep up my strength and

get out of here. I'm a highly trained police detective and I won't sit around weeping all the time. I sat up and went over to the chair. *Pull yourself together for fucks sake, Janey. Get with the programme and form a plan to escape.* I took the food out of the plastic bag but held my nose while I ate the egg sandwiches. Really, does anybody eat these by choice? The plastic bags were the only things I had. How could I use these to regain my freedom? I mulled this over while I made sure I chewed my apple to a pulp while I thought about this and also to make the minor activity last as long as possible. Last of all I savoured my chocolate. I smiled as I thought again about Craig and his wee smiley face.

Chapter Thirty-Six

Meera looked surprised when Tim and Angus walked into the mortuary with Bear who was holding his arm.

"My goodness, did you hire an a cappella group to liven up our afternoon?" she asked her colleague. "Bear, what's the matter with your arm?"

Bear explained what had happened and submitted to a further examination of his wound by Meera and David.

"A guy sliced me while he was trying to escape. I suppose if I'd let him go sooner, he wouldn't have got the blade out."

"No guarantee of that. Let me look." Meera removed the dressing Rachael had applied. "Rachael did a good job. It does look deep, though. I think you should go to the hospital and get it checked."

"No thanks, Meera. I'm only here so you can look at my arm. Tim thought, if you saw the cut, it might help you work out if the knife used was similar to the slicing on our victims. But after this, I really just want to go home and go to sleep."

"Is your tetanus jab up to date?"

"Yes. I'm all set."

"I think if it's not the same knife, it's a remarkably similar one. Look at the wound. What do you think, David?"

"I see what you mean. And this is the knife?"

"Yes, he dropped it when I fought back and Rachael lifted it with a tissue, but I don't think there'll be any DNA on it, he was wearing gloves."

"It'll still be worth sending it to the forensic lab, they can use a minute amount of DNA," David said.

"Do you want me to put a stitch in your arm, Bear?"

"Does it really need it?"

"The wound may heal a little faster and hurt a bit less. I

promise I'll give you a local anaesthetic before getting out my needle and thread."

"Go on then." Bear grimaced as Meera tended to his arm.

"You're not good with blood, are you, big man?" Tim said.

"Especially mine."

"Can we leave this with you, Meera?" Tim pointed to the knife. "Angus wants to take Bear home and then drop me off at Rachael's and I'll just stop there while our highland friend here does some investigation into Jane's brother, Donny."

"No problem, Tim. How's Gillian keeping since Zelay was killed."

"Not well. It's not just Zelay. She'd met the judge that was killed too. I've tried to help raise her spirits, but nothing seems to work.

"We were meant to be going on holiday to the Seychelles, but she's determined to travel back to Ukraine with Zelay's body when it is released to his family. Apparently, I'm not included."

Meera looked puzzled. "Well, I suppose everybody deals with grief in their own way. But if you need company to go to the Seychelles, I'm sure Hunter wouldn't miss me for a couple of weeks."

"And if it's all the same to you, Meera, I'm equally sure he would. I have my sergeant's exams coming up, I don't want to get into the Boss's bad books." Tim grinned and then turned to Bear, "come on, big man, let's get you home, shall we?"

"Is that it? Thanks, Meera, it didn't hurt at all."

"It will when that local anaesthetic wears off."

When Angus and Tim dropped Bear off at his Marchmont flat, Mel was already home. Tim explained what had happened and helped his friend onto the couch. He laughed as Bear began to groan and complain.

"Meera gave him a local anaesthetic to numb the pain while she put in the stitches. It's probably wearing off."

"I doubt it. He's just chancing his arm." Mel laughed.

"That's not funny," Bear moaned.

"Any word about Jane?"

"Not yet."

"Oh God. Rachael must be at the end of her tether. The

longer she's missing, the worse it could be. What if she's..."

"She's not," Tim said.

"Of course she's not, silly of me," Mel said. "Now, let me take care of the invalid. If you hear anything, Tim, will you let me know?"

Tim nodded and turned to go back to the car. "Poor old Angus will have to search the property registers alone; I've got to go back and be with Rache."

"What's he looking for?"

"Jane's brother's flat in Dundee Street."

"Poor lad, it's a long street. Look, I can help him. I'll search the register from here. What's the guy's name?"

"Donald Smith."

"Really? Just my luck. Tell Angus I'll take the even numbers and he can do the odd. Do we know when he bought the flat?"

"Not a fucking clue. I suppose you just start with today and work back."

"Why did I open my big mouth?" Mel smiled at Tim and saw him out. "Send Rache my love."

Tim nodded and made his way down the stairs two at a time. He told Angus about Mel's offer of help and watched the huge grin spread over his friend's face.

***

Angus phoned DI Jallow to explain his extended absence and what he planned to do next. The DI agreed he would be better doing his investigations in Edinburgh rather than travelling back to Gartcosh.

He drove back to the station to begin looking up the records of property purchases. He made himself a large mug of coffee before settling down at the computer to begin his search.

What a boring job. Thank goodness Mel had offered to help, but even with that he did not think this was going to be an easy task, unless the man had bought his flat recently, which Angus thought unlikely. Why did the man's name have to be Smith? Why couldn't it be the one who had been adopted and used Bean?

Chapter Thirty-Seven

"Why do you have to stay with Rachael? Can't she look after herself? She's a bloody police detective, after all. She's trained to deal with difficult situations. I'm not, and I'm dealing with Zelay's murder all on my own. You should be here, comforting me, Tim."

"Gillian, darling, I know you're grieving, but Zelay was your colleague, not your lover, and Rachael's partner is missing. We don't know what danger she may be in. Be reasonable."

There was a slight pause before Gillian replied. "Zelay and I were close, you know that, and from where I'm sitting, it feels like my partner is missing too. It's not me who's being unreasonable, it's you, Tim."

Tim sighed. "Well why don't you pack a bag and come and stay here for a while? The bed in their spare room is a double and playing *Monopoly* is much more fun with three."

"I hate *Monopoly.*"

The line went dead. Tim tried to call back, but Gillian's phone went straight to voicemail. He looked at his mobile, thought about phoning the house phone and then decided against it. Let her stew for a while. Rachael's need was greater.

"Was that Gillian?"

"Yes, she's still pretty upset about Zelay and can't imagine what stress you're going through. She sends her love."

"She's a dear. Do you think she's the one for you?"

"You never know."

"You do believe Jane's still alive, don't you, Tim? I mean her abduction may have nothing to do with the murders. What would I ever do if anything happened to her?"

"Come on, Rache. I need you strong. Shall we go out for a jog?"

"Because you know how much I like running." Rachael blew her nose and looked up at Tim.

"Well, fair point. Shall we go to the shops and get something we both like to eat?"

"That's more or less what Bear and I were doing and look what happened then. Maybe I'm doomed to stay in here forever. Scared, miserable and alone."

"I doubt it, and you're not alone. Come on, we'll take a walk around the neighbourhood and check there are no baddies looking to take us out."

"Don't joke." Rachael pulled her jacket on and scowled at Tim. "Let's go before I change my mind."

They walked around Bruntsfield and picked up some groceries. Meat from *Christie's*, homemade bread from *Bakery Andante* and fruit and vegetables from the crowd-funded grocery store, *Dig-In*. Tim realised that Rachael was beginning to relax when she insisted on going into *Coco's* and bought an inordinate amount of chocolate.

"We'll need something to wash that down," Tim said and led the way to the *181 deli* where they picked up wine, beer and a variety of soft drinks.

"This is getting heavy. Let's get back to the flat."

"Good idea. And as I'm doing the heavy lifting, you can do the cooking."

"As if it was ever going to be any other way, Tim Myerscough. You are cheeky." Suddenly Tim saw Rachael's attitude change. "What do you think Janey is getting to eat? Do you think she's being starved? Oh God, just bring her home to me."

***

When they got back to the flat, Rachael put the groceries away and Tim noticed he had a missed call from Gillian on his phone. He debated whether to call back. He was still upset by their previous exchange. Then, having thought about it, he decided she was probably even more upset than he was. He called back.

"What took you so long?"

"Hello to you too, Gillian."

"I'm sorry. It's just that one of the papers has published a link between those murder victims. The connection is Edinburgh University. It's terrifying. And I know them all."

"What?"

"I know them all. I had never made the connection, but the two other women Beatrice and Dolores were on that jury with me. I didn't make the connection before. I was too wrapped up with Zelay's murder."

"You mean the one where Lady Munro heard the case?"

"Well, I haven't been on any other juries, have I? Oh Tim, I'm so frightened. You should be here with me."

We're back to that, he thought.

"Where does the University come into it? And where does Zelay fit in? You're not talking a lot of sense, Gillian."

"Each of the victims is connected to Edinburgh University. Including Zelay."

"That's not surprising, they all lived in Edinburgh and it's a huge university. I honestly think the papers are just making headlines but come over here if you want to be with me."

"You're not coming home? Not even with this? I work at Edinburgh University, you know."

"I'm perfectly well aware of where you work, Gillian. 11,000 other people who have not been killed also work there. But if you want to share this gem of information with Angus, please feel free to do so."

"You are being so horrible, Tim. I'm scared."

"Too scared to come on holiday with me but not too scared to travel with a corpse halfway across the world."

She cut the call. Tim sat and stared at his phone then he heard Rachael call through to him.

"Call her back. Don't leave it like that. Tell her to come over and I'll make a meal for all three of us."

Tim dialled the house phone and was relieved when he heard Gillian's voice.

Chapter Thirty-Eight

Rachael was glad when she opened her door and found Gillian standing there looking sheepish and holding a newspaper.

"I can't stay late," Gillian said. "I'm giving a guest lecture at Glasgow University tomorrow."

"Don't worry about that. It's just good to see you." Rachael dragged her friend into the flat and left her to chat alone with Tim under the pretence of going to open a bottle of wine.

When they had finished speaking, Rachael quickly served the tagliatelle dish she had made. It was veggie with Gillian in mind and the spinach, corn, pine nuts and parmesan made a good meal with the fresh crusty bread.

Rachael was aware that they were all quiet during the meal. She guessed nobody wanted to say the wrong thing. When they had finished the food and the wine, Rachael put on a pot of coffee and watched as Tim and Gillian gathered up the dishes and loaded them into the dishwasher. She sat and flicked through Gillian's newspaper and pretended to be unable to hear the conciliatory talk between the other two.

Suddenly, she stopped flicking. She stared at the photograph on page nine. There was a man, who if he had been a woman would have looked just like Jane. She took it over to the window and examined the page in the light. Automatically she looked down into the back green where the stalker usually stood. There was nobody there.

Tim looked away from Gillian. "What's so interesting in the local paper today?"

"Nothing. I only bought it because I needed change."

"Rache, what has caught your attention?"

Rachael looked up and pointed to the photograph. "Who does he remind you of?"

She handed the paper to Tim, and he looked at the photograph.

"I see what you mean. Gillian, what do you think?" He handed across the paper.

"What an amazing resemblance. That could almost be Jane."

"That's what I thought," Tim said. "What does it say about him?"

Rachael looked up at Tim. "The article says his name is Craig Smith."

"Jane's other brother's name. It could be a coincidence, Rache."

"And it could be the man who knows where she is."

Tim spread the paper out so they could all see it and he read out the short article:

For the first time in eleven years, the award for the quickest dissection of a cow in the whole of Scotland has come back to Edinburgh. Craig Smith, (28) master butcher at Robert Wilson's (Ltd) Butchers in the Grassmarket, Edinburgh, won the title by completing the dissection of the cow 32 seconds ahead of last year's champion, Henry Devine of Largs. Craig said, "It is a great honour to have won the title and brought the trophy back to Edinburgh after all this time. All the lads were great competitors, and it was touch and go at the end as to whether Henry or I would take it. I'll be back next year to try to keep the trophy here in the capital."

"It could just be a coincidence. Newspapers don't have the best pictures in the world, Rache," Gillian said.

"But I have to check. Look, he's the right age. I have to see him, don't you understand?"

"Of course, but he could be a very dangerous man."

"She won't be going on her own," Tim said softly. "Rachael, why don't we call Angus, and he can have a look at the article online and let DCI Mackay and the other chiefs who are heading the both the murder investigation and Jane's disappearance know what you've found. Then Angus and I can go to the shop and have a word with him."

"I'm coming too."

"That's probably not a good idea."

"I'm going to the shop to see him. I'll go either with you and Angus or on my own, but I'm going to be there."

***

Rachael phoned Angus. He called back after he had looked at the photo and agreed with Rachael that from the picture in the paper the man looked extremely like Jane. He forwarded the information onto the office in Gartcosh, and DI Jallow gave him instructions to take Tim with him and interview the man.

Angus also listened quietly as his boss gave specific instructions that Rachael should be nowhere in the vicinity while he and Tim carried out their investigations. He acknowledged her instructions, ended the call, and shook his head. DI Jallow had just wasted a great deal of breath, but he had no intentions of telling her that. He already knew her too well to try to argue the point.

Chapter Thirty-Nine

I had slept again, I didn't know if it had been night or day, but there was little else to do. I sat on the chair and gazed at the floor instead of doing my exercises. I thought I might do them later. I knew I had to stay fit, strong, and motivated, and I had to find a way to get out, to find a way back to Rachael.

Was I ever going to get home? I would even have agreed to Rachael getting that dog she kept banging on about, if that's what it took to return to our home again. I sat on the bed and fiddled with a plastic bag. How could I use this to help me escape? Plastic bags were all I had.

Maybe if I could speak to him and tell him about my life and what I was missing. Perhaps then he would take pity on me and let me go. It wasn't as if I'd ever seen him, so I couldn't identify him. I decided I would try that.

The next time the door opened, and the new bag was handed in, I said, "Hello. What's in my sandwich today?"

There was no reply.

"I don't like to complain, but I really don't like egg mayonnaise, I never have."

"I know but it's all they had left," he said.

"How do you know? How can you possibly know that I don't like egg sandwiches?"

He hesitated. "I've been watching you, haven't I?"

"But not when I'm eating. Why have you been watching me? I don't even know who you are."

"That's the way it has to be. And you must stay here, until this is all over and you're able to go back to your life safely. I'm just looking out for you."

"This is a funny way of looking out for me. What on earth are you talking about? What has to be over? You're making no sense at all. Just let me go home, please."

"Not yet, Jane. Not yet."

"You know my name. How do you know my name?"

"I told you, I've been watching you." He put the bag down in front of me.

I looked at it and then up at him again.

"Chicken."

"What?"

"They're chicken sandwiches today."

I heard him close the door quietly and lock it quickly. Still, I had no plans to rush him that day. I was too miserable. I felt completely defeated. There was nothing I could do about that. He seemed determined that I was in some sort of danger and that he was keeping me safe. He seemed anxious to keep me here, inside, away from whatever or whoever he thought would hurt me. I hoped he'd offer me a shower tomorrow. That would make me feel better and maybe it would cheer me up.

***

He had only found out about the danger by chance and had saved up his leave when he realised what was going on. He couldn't save all of them, but he would try to look out for Jane.

Chapter Forty

Amar was irritated with Jallow. He felt he had been side-tracked by the long drink of water highlander new boy. Why should the boss put so much trust in Angus and leave him doing dreaded paperwork with Brian and Judy? Just because Angus lived in Edinburgh. Just because the Craig Smith he interviewed, wasn't the right Craig Smith. It was hardly his fault.

"Amar, have you found anything else that links our murder victims?" DI Jallow asked.

"Nothing that's going to help us much. Lady Munro went to a charity fashion show run by Dolores Cline."

"Really? That's interesting. Judy, can you find out who else was there and give me a list of attendees. Amar, you keep looking."

"I found one thing, boss." Brian walked over to the DI. Beatrice Dalgleish was the foreman of the jury in a recent case tried before Lady Munro."

"Oh really? What was the case about?"

"Little girl. Died in the dentist's chair. Had to get all her first teeth pulled. Young single mother, they're all the same, aren't they?"

"Are they? My mother was a single mother," DI Jallow said sharply. "What happened to the kid?"

Brian blushed. "Sorry boss, no offence intended. Too much anaesthetic. She was a tiny wee thing, and the dentist calculated her weight in kilos, not pounds."

"It must have been terrible for the family. Losing a kiddie like that."

"Yes, boss. They were furious about the judgement and the sentence. He wasn't done for murder, but negligence and he got less than six years. He'll be out in less than three with good behaviour."

"Hmm, but he won't ever work as a dentist again."

"No, he won't. Not that the family seemed to care about that. They campaigned for a longer sentence, to have the judge removed from the bench and for the jury members to be banned from ever serving on a jury again," Brian said. "They're in some paper or other almost every week."

"Right, Judy, you check out the family. Brian, you get on to everyone else who was connected to the case and Amar, I want you to continue working on any other connections between our murder victims." Regina Jallow turned on her heels to leave.

"Boss, you do think we'll find Jane alive, don't you?" Judy asked.

"I bloody well hope so, Judy. I really do. You all keep working on this. We know our perpetrator is Jane's brother, so it does seem highly likely that her disappearance is connected to the murder investigations."

"Yes, boss, but how?"

"Oh, for God's sake, Amar, you're a detective. Detect. I'm going to phone Angus and see how he and the local lads are getting on in Edinburgh."

"Oh, I've just had a text from my brother, he didn't win the gold medal for that surgery course he was going for during his study rotation."

"That's a shame," Judy said. "Who did?"

"Troy Bean. Wait a minute, that's Jane's youngest brother."

"Yes, it is, I remember the unusual name," Brian said. "Imagine calling your son Troy Bean, poor bugger."

"Well, his parents can't help their last name being Bean." Amar said.

"And at least they didn't call him jelly or baked," Judy laughed.

"Or green," Brian joined in.

"Shut up you two. I'm going to speak to the boss."

"Speak to me about what?"

"I've just had a text from my brother and Jane's youngest brother that Angus and I met at Glasgow Uni won the gold medal in surgery."

"Very nice for him. Angus is going with one of the local boys to interview a butcher with the same name as the middle brother. I hope they have better luck than you did."

Amar shot a glance at Judy. She was blushing as she walked quietly back to her desk to begin an investigation into the attendees at the fashion show and the child victim's family.

**

"What have you found out, Judy?"

"Oh, hello boss, I didn't see you there. It's quite funny, the two groups of people couldn't be more different."

"In what way?"

"The people at the charity event were the great and the good, the family certainly does not fall into that category."

"Show me the charity list." Judy handed the list to DI Jallow. "And this came from the fashion house's records?"

"Yes, I got it from Ms Cline's PA. She's still a PA within the company. They've taken on a new senior designer."

"I see what you mean, judges, lawyers, doctors, novelists, film producers, ambassadors and consular officials. A high net worth gathering indeed. And Beatrice Dalgleish as well as lady Munro attended? Interesting. Any criminal records amongst the guests?"

"Nothing apart from a few parking tickets, boss."

"What about the child's family?"

"Single mother of a single mother if you see what I mean. The child's mother is a classroom assistant in a primary school. Crazy about kids. Her mother is a nurse and her uncle and grandfather run their own plumbing business."

"As plumbers they probably earn twice as much as some of the authors at that charity gathering, Dolores might have been better to invite them."

"Perhaps boss."

"Have you managed to find out anything about the child's father?"

"No, she went by the mother's last name, Hourston. I was

just about to see it I could get a copy of the birth certificate."

"Keep me posted. Brian, how are your investigations going?"

"You asked me to look into the people who had a connection with the child's case."

"Yes, what did you find?"

"The usual clerk of court who sat in with Lady Munro was on holiday, so the clerk filling in was a Rose Brown. The stenographer was the usual chap, Eric King."

"Are both of these individuals regular employees within the Scottish Courts?"

"Yes, boss. But there are a couple of other interesting things. Jane was the only member of Police Scotland to give evidence."

"Oh really? Keep digging then. Amar, and tell me you've found something else that connects all our victims."

"Unfortunately nothing yet, boss. But there is an interesting thing, not only was Beatrice Dalgleish the foreman of the jury, but Dolores Cline was on that jury too."

"And Lady Munro was the judge. Was that university professor, Zelay Sheptytsky, on the jury?"

"No, boss."

"Was he at the fashion show, Judy?"

"No, boss, that's a name I wouldn't miss."

"So where does he fit in. Could he be the father?"

"I'm still looking for the birth certificate."

"But Jane gave evidence. You know, this might be beginning to make sense. Judy, find that birth certificate and Amar, check if any other jurors or witnesses worked with Professor Sheptytsky at the University of Edinburgh or if we've missed anything else that he has in common with the other victims."

"And me, boss?" Brian asked.

"Make us all a cuppa, will you Brian?"

163

Chapter Forty-One

"Angus, if you're going to interview the butcher with Tim, leave me to do the rest of the property search for Dundee Street," Mel said. "No, I haven't got a problem keeping the big man in. I've hidden the front door keys in my knickers." She laughed. "Yes, it's bloody uncomfortable, but he doesn't know they're there, so he's never going to find them. At least not until he's feeling a lot better. Let me know how it goes with the butcher."

"Aye, will do Mel." Angus was laughing as he, Tim, and Rachael got into the car.

"What's so funny?" Rachael asked angrily.

Angus explained about Mel's keys, and they were all laughing on the drive to the Grassmarket.

"Parking here is always a nightmare," Tim said.

"Especially when you drive a huge BMW7 series like this," Angus said.

"If that's a complaint, next time, you can walk."

"Not a complaint, just an observation. Look, there's a space."

Tim spun into the only space they could see, and the three detectives sat in silence.

"Well, are we going to do this?" Rachael asked.

"Yes, but you can't be with us," Tim said.

"Why don't you go in first and see if you recognise anybody behind the counter as the man in the photo, the one who attacked Bear or even Jane's stalker?" Angus suggested.

"Aren't they the same person?" Rachael asked.

"Possibly, but we don't have any forensics back on the knife yet and you've only seen the stalker at a distance through the kitchen window. Just buy a couple of steaks or a pound of mince or something and keep your eyes open."

"I suppose I could try that. I'll go in and you wait here."

"We'll go and get a drink in the Beehive," said Tim. He pointed to the pub across the road. "Meet us in there."

Rachael nodded and walked towards the shop. She walked slowly with her head down and tears in her eyes. What if Jane was already dead? Was this all a waste of time? What would she do if she recognised a man behind the counter? What would she do if he recognised her? That would be worse. At least there was a line of customers, so she would have to have to wait. Excellent. She could pull herself together and study the faces of each of the butchers in turn without being too obvious about it.

The little old lady at the front of the queue seemed to be buying everything in tiny quantities.

"Two sausages, Ernie, a quarter of mince and one pork chop."

"No bacon today, Mildred?"

"Oh, go on, but just two slices."

"Aye, no problem, dear."

Rachael began to listen to the man behind Mildred in line. She saw he was looking at a large leg of lamb.

"Good morning, Mr Walker. Entertaining at the weekend are we, sir?"

"Yes indeed, Verity. I need four fillet steaks, and that large goose for the family, and I'll take the biggest leg of lamb you've got. It's my birthday on Sunday, so we're having a few people round to help me celebrate."

"Sounds lovely, Mr Walker."

Then Rachael's attention was drawn to the man who came through from the back shop to serve the man in front of her. She couldn't help staring. He looked even more like Jane in real life than he had in the picture.

"What can I get for you?" he asked.

"Didn't I see you in the *Evening News*?"

Rachael saw the butcher's cheeks colour. His colleagues whistled and cheered to add to the man's discomfort.

"Yes, you did, I won a competition."

"It's Craig, isn't it? Well done you." The man shook the butcher's hand. So can you cut me six pork chops, three sirloin steaks, half a kilo of sausages and a homemade steak pie."

Rachael continued to stare at the man. She felt sick. She was shaking. She couldn't stand there any longer. She gasped and ran from the shop. A car missed her by inches and the driver sat on his horn. Rachael paid no attention. She looked up only to check where the Beehive was and charged through the door.

"He's there," she sobbed. "I saw him. It has to be him."

She sat crying while Tim comforted her, and Angus brought her over a large mug of tea.

"We'll just sit for a little while until you're calmer, then we'll go and have a chat with the award-winning Craig Smith," Tim said

"I just hope he's the right Craig Smith." Rachael sniffed.

Chapter Forty-Two

Bear lay on the sofa in the living room. His activities alternated between playing Fortnite, watching sport, and drinking coffee. As long as he didn't move much, his arm felt fine, but if he had to do anything that involved using his arm, like cooking, washing dishes, vacuuming, or answering the door, he made sure Mel knew how much pain he suffered.

"You are a real hypochondriac, Winston Zewedu," Mel said, giving him his full Sunday name. "I really think that wound is deeper than you noticed, and you should have gone to the hospital to get it properly seen to. You would also have been given proper painkillers."

"I suppose."

"Suppose nothing. If I had known how many paracetamols you would be chomping, I'd have bought shares in the company."

"You're not funny, Mel. It's really sore if I use my arm, but Meera put a couple of stitches in it to close the wound."

"Aye, but it's long as well as deep."

"At least he didn't get Rache, and we got the knife. Forensics are examining that now. I don't suppose you'd be thinking of making a bite of lunch?"

"I was, but I think I've found Donny's flat. Trust him to buy at the far end of the street."

"You've found it? That's amazing. You need to phone Angus."

"I think he's interviewing the butcher, Craig Smith, with Tim today. I don't want to interrupt. I'm going to call MIT at Gartcosh, though, because I want to share this information with the team right away. Can you wait for half an hour and then I'll make us lunch? It'll be time for you to have your next painkillers by then too, if you need them."

"No problem, pet. And I'm fairly sure I will be howling for painkillers by then."

He sat with the sound down on the sports channel while Mel made her call. He was happy for her because she sounded so excited. Perhaps this would help to solve the spree of murders, or Jane's disappearance, or both. If Bear were honest with himself, as long as they found Jane safe and well, he would be content.

"I spoke to a DC, Amar Patel his name was, he sounded extremely pleased with the news and he was thrilled that I phoned Gartcosh rather than Angus. He sounded fed up that he was stuck in the incident room while Angus was out interviewing a potential suspect."

"How did this poor butcher get from winning a competition for his company to potential suspect? That's a bit rough on him."

"Well, when you think about it, if he can cut up a cow with ease, he would surely know where to slice a person's neck to kill them quickly," Mel said.

"That's nuts. It's a long way from being good at your job as a butcher to being a killer. Think about it, not all mechanics are car thieves, are they?" He slammed his injured arm down onto his lap to make his point and yelled loudly in pain.

"You don't worry about any of that. I'll make lunch. Amar is coming over from Gartcosh this afternoon with his colleague, DC Judy Marsh, to check out the flat that I think belongs to Jane's brother. I hope the address I gave him is the right one."

Chapter Forty-Three

I was becoming increasingly disoriented, sitting staring at the walls. I didn't know if it was night or day. I had to get out. How were a few plastic bags going to help me win my freedom? I could hear him walking about outside the door from time to time, but he only opened the door to hand in my supplies. The room smelled bad because of the bucket, and I knew I was depressed.

The key turned, and he put his head around the door.

"Want a shower?"

"Yes, definitely."

"I'll wash your clothes same as last time if you hand them out."

It was probably as much as he had ever said to me. I walked in front of him along the dark corridor to the shower room. After the door locked, I undressed and knocked when I was ready to hand out my things. I didn't like the thought of him touching my knickers and my bra, but what choice did I have? I didn't feel fresh anyway, but I'd smell pretty rancid if he hadn't washed my clothes.

I took the advantage of a long hot shower, then sat on the loo wrapped up in my towel, and thought about how to get out of this place.

It was clear my captor had no intention of hurting me. He just seemed to want to keep me in this place, like an exhibit or a trophy. But I couldn't cope locked up in a big cupboard eating sandwiches for much longer. Rachael must surely think the worst. I had to get out.

Then I looked at the soap. It wasn't a big bar, and it wasn't new, but it was at that slimy stage. When I lived on my own, I always hated when the soap got to be like that. Now I'm with

Rachael, we are wasteful with soap, though not with most other things. Still, when the soap gets slimy, it goes out and we start a new bar.

I picked up the slimy soap and it slipped out of my hand onto the floor. I looked at the mark it left on the floor, and I began to form a plan. I smiled. I don't know how long I'd been sitting daydreaming and working out my escape. Probably longer than it felt then I heard a knock on the door. He unlocked the door from the outside and handed my clothes to me.

"Give me a knock on the door when you're ready to come out."

I didn't think my plan would work from the bathroom, so I got dressed and hid the soap in my pocket, then I allowed him to march me back along the corridor to the windowless room. At least it smelled better. He had emptied and disinfected the bucket. I wondered where he emptied it when I was in the bathroom, but I decided that was not my problem.

There was another flask of tea and a bag with a packet of sandwiches, a bottle of water, a bag of crisps, an apple and one of the same little bars of chocolate. Everything else varied, but the type of chocolate was always the same. I couldn't help wondering why. Had he got a bulk buy on this chocolate? I couldn't help smiling.

Then I began tying plastic bags tightly together into a firm cord. I also needed to work out how to make the floor slippery and keep it that way until the next time he came in. After the soap dried, it just got sticky. It didn't stay slippery for long. I tugged on my cord of plastic bags to make sure it was as strong as it could be and then sat down on the floor to lick my chocolate and think things through.

As I sat quietly, I realised I could hear him outside wandering up and down, but his footsteps weren't as noisy when he was coming to me, because I was rarely aware that he was coming until I heard the key in the lock. That meant I would always have a few seconds to wet the soap with my bottle of water and make the floor slippery. Good. Now, if I tied one end of my cord to the leg of the bed and the other firmly around the pipe on the wall beside the door, that may work. I had one bag left. I sat and looked at it, and then I had a lightbulb moment, I'd put the extra bag over his head as he fell and make my escape, but there was no doubt I'd have to be quick.

He walked about outside, but the change in footsteps never came. It seemed he wasn't coming back into my room. Then it dawned on me. I'd had a shower, my clothes were clean, my bucket had been emptied, and he'd handed in food. He had no reason to come back in. I lay back onto the bed and stared at the ceiling until I fell asleep.

***

I don't know what woke me, but I came to suddenly. There was shouting coming from somewhere. Loud angry voices. They were arguing and I heard my name. I had no idea what was going on, but I thought I should get ready. I wet the soap with all the water left in my bottle, made the floor slippery and crouched beside the door.

It crashed open with a bang. Two men tripped over my cord, slipped on the soap, and landed in a heap beside me. I didn't need my extra bag. I just had to get out of there.

The door to the flat was open, probably because of the visitor who was clearly unwelcome and had been arguing with my captor. What if it were a copper? I didn't want to take time to check. I ran out of the flat and down the stairs to make my escape. I shouted for help, but there was nobody around. No problem, I just needed to find a phone box. Why are there no phone boxes anymore?

Shit. I could hear one of the men shouting after me.

"Stop. Stop, you bitch, I told you to stop."

Yes, I could see how that might work.

"You sprained my bloody ankle, but I'll get you, and you'll be sorry."

I didn't think so, and I definitely was not sorry. I just kept running.

Chapter Forty-Four

Gillian enjoyed travelling, and whenever she was invited to lecture, the further the venue was from Edinburgh, the more enthusiasm she would show when accepting. Today's trip was only to The University of Glasgow, but it allowed her to travel by train across the country and escape Edinburgh with its shadow of Zelay's death. It also allowed her to leave home behind her. She was angry with Tim for agreeing to stay at Jane and Rachael's flat, especially now Bear was nursing his arm, and all the responsibility had been taken over by Tim.

She sat and gazed out of the window of the train. Her train was at the front end of the platform, and she saw a young man running along to reach it. The doors of the train had locked, ready for departure, but he kept going. He was shouting, but to no avail, the train took off without him.

Gillian saw him. She didn't need to hear him to know what he had said. He swore, stopped running, and then held his knees before he looked up. It felt like he looked directly at her.

It was hard to imagine why he was so upset. The trains between Edinburgh and Glasgow were every quarter of an hour. The man would not be so terribly delayed. Still, when she thought about it, missing a train was always irritating.

The train manger checked all the tickets and, after putting hers securely back in her purse, Gillian rummaged through her briefcase to make sure she had all her notes. Her main expertise was in eastern European languages, Russian, Ukrainian, Uzbek, Georgian, Slovakian, Slovenian, Czech, and German was thrown in for good measure. She had always liked to talk and making herself understood as her parents worked their way around the region, teaching English as a foreign language.

Now she spent most of her time teaching the eastern languages to British students, and today she had been invited to Glasgow to discuss with one of their language professors the differences and similarities between Czech and Slovakian. Special reference was to be made to nuances and changes that had developed since the countries separated. It should be an interesting morning because her audience was due to be a group of post-graduate students studying not only languages but also philology and linguistics. She smiled as she ran over the beginning of her talk in her head. She would leave lots of time for questions because this would be an inquisitive group.

The man with a trolley came through the carriage, and Gillian chose a coffee. She sipped it while she ran through her presentation one last time. It wasn't long before the train arrived at Glasgow's Queen Street Station, and from there she took a taxi to the university.

***

"I've rarely seen the students so engaged, Gillian. Would you like to grab a bite of lunch in the cafeteria with me?" the host lecturer, Petra Karimov, asked.

"Thanks. I'm glad you think they enjoyed the talk, Petra. I'd love to join you for lunch. That was an interesting discussion afterwards too, wasn't it?"

"Yes, I found it fascinating that the students studying the different disciplines all took something particular to their course from what you had to say."

"I noticed that. I hoped they might. Now, you said something about lunch?"

"Follow me. The food in the canteen isn't too bad, and it also means that any students who still want to speak to you will be able to come over and chat. Or would you rather go somewhere else to avoid that?"

"Not at all. Lead the way," Gillian said.

Gillian and Petra both chose the vegetarian pasta dish and a side salad and washed it all down with a glass of water. While they sat and chatted, a few of the students stopped at their table to thank Gillian for her talk.

"Do you go back to Eastern Europe often?" asked an earnest young man.

"I'm going back to Ukraine shortly. A former colleague was a professor at the University, and I'm going to visit in his honour."

"That must be Professor Scheptytsky. I heard about his murder. Dreadful. Have they found out who did it yet?"

"Not yet."

"Why would anybody murder a university professor? It's not as if any of you have any money."

"That's certainly true," Petra said. "If you have nothing further to discuss with Dr Pearson about her lecture, perhaps you can excuse us while we go to my room for a quiet coffee."

"Yes, of course. Thank you again, Dr Pearson."

As Gillian followed Petra out of the cafeteria, she noticed there was another person staring at her intently. She looked at him and he looked away quickly, but not before she recognised him as the man who had missed the train.

Chapter Forty-Five

"Are you feeling better, Rachael," Angus said. "Would you rather Tim stayed with you? I can go and speak to this butcher guy on my own."

"No, really, it's fine. I just don't know what came over me. I got a bit of a shock when I saw how strong the family resemblance was between him and Jane, I suppose."

"Well, they say everybody has a doppelgänger somewhere, don't they?"

"I wouldn't like to be your doppelgänger, Angus," Tim laughed. "Imagine me as a ginger."

"Don't be like that. It's not kind to mock the afflicted," Rachael said.

"At least we got a smile out of you, Rache. You stay here and we'll see what we can find out," Angus said. He stood up and began to move towards the door.

"When we get back, I'll treat us all to lunch. The menu's not bad." Tim smiled and followed Angus towards the door.

***

When they crossed the road and looked into the butcher's shop, they were surprised that the queue Rachael had had to join earlier was gone.

"Quiet today?" Tim asked the man behind the counter.

"Always gets quieter around this time in the morning. It's after the early birds and before the lunchtime rush. Anyway, what can I do you for, gents?"

"We're looking for Craig Smith. Is he in today?"

"Aye, he's just having a wazz. Who wants to know?"

Tim and Angus showed their IDs. "DCs Myerscough and

McKenzie."

"Did I hear you taking my name in vain, Ernie?"

"Her Majesty's boys in blue want a word, Craig."

"Oh yes. How can I help you?"

"Is there somewhere private we could speak, Mr Smith?"

"Only the back shop. Provided you boys aren't too squeamish."

"We'll manage," Angus said.

"Mr Smith, may I just establish your identity, before we go any further?" Tim said softly.

"Go ahead."

"You are Craig Smith. Any middle names?"

"No. My parents couldn't even give me a home, never mind a middle name."

"Can you please confirm your date of birth?"

The man did so but looked increasingly uncomfortable.

"And your address, Mr Smith."

He told them and then began shifting from one foot to the other.

"Do you have any brothers or sisters?" Angus asked.

"For goodness' sake, what is all this about?"

"Just answer the question, Craig," Angus said.

Ernie popped his head around the door. "Everything okay, Craig?" he asked.

"Yes, but I'm not saying nothing more until these cops tell me what this is all about."

"I think we better continue this conversation at the station, Mr Smith," Tim said. "It will be more private and will allow us to ask our questions without anybody overhearing."

"Anything to get out of buying lunch." Angus smiled. "I'll go and get Rachael."

Rachael looked up as Angus walked in. "We're not lunching, are we?"

"No sorry, Rache. The things Tim'll do to keep his wallet in his pocket."

"That's not really fair. He's generous to a fault." Rachael picked up her jacket and followed Angus to the door. "It's a real pity, they've got Hunter's Chicken on the menu."

"Ha, very funny. We'll need to come back for that. When Jane's back, let's come for dinner and have Hunter's Chicken."

"Not when, Angus. If."

***

Angus watched Rachael walk towards the incident room in Fettes. He thought it would probably do her good to chat to her Edinburgh colleagues and friends. He swung around and followed Tim as he guided Craig Smith along the corridor to interview room one.

Without being asked, Craig moved to sit in the chair at the far side of the table. It was clear to Angus that this wasn't the first time Craig had been in a room like this.

Craig stared bleakly at his surroundings. The room was small and dark. The only window had bars across it and was almost at the height of the ceiling. Craig was tall and slim, but not tall enough to see out of it. The smell in the interview room was, like all other interview rooms, stale. It didn't seem to matter how much disinfectant the cleaners used, or how much air-freshener the officers sprayed around after the rooms were used, the smell of dirt, body odour and farts always lingered. This room was no different.

"Now Craig, let's start at the very beginning," Tim said. He explained that the interview would be recorded both by tape and on film and introduced those in the room.

"But why am I here?" Craig whined.

"We think you may be able to help us with our enquiries."

"So, I'm a witness? I've not been arrested."

"No, you have certainly not been arrested. You're free to leave at any time. We would just like to ask you a few questions."

"Well, get on with it. Can I have a cup of tea?"

Tim looked at the PC who was standing at the door and nodded. "Could you get us a tea and two coffees please, Neil, and whatever you're having."

"You're too kind."

"Now back to business, Craig. What's your full name?"

Chapter Forty-Six

I just kept running. I didn't look back. They told me at school that if you looked back, you'd be slower. I had to get away before the two of them pulled themselves apart and started chasing me.

When I pulled open the door at the foot of the stairs and bounded into the daylight, I could hardly open my eyes. The light felt so bright, I couldn't see properly but I had to keep running. I knew it must be early because of the position of the sun, but I couldn't get distracted by that, I had to get away.

Even with the exercises I had done, I could feel my muscles cramping. I don't know how long I'd been kept prisoner, probably not for as long as it felt, but I hadn't been doing my regular runs and my legs were complaining. Still, I mustn't slow down.

A telephone box, you don't see many of them now. I opened the door. It was vandalised and broken beyond repair. Of course it was. Bugger! And now I had really slowed up. I could hear them behind me shouting and swearing.

"Stop, bitch!"

"Come back!"

Like that was going to happen. I couldn't help it. I was terrified and didn't follow my own advice. I turned round to see how far back they were. Bad idea. There were two of them pounding along the street after me. My tall, thin captor was chasing after the other one who had arrived on the scene. The captor seemed to be more anxious to catch up with the other one than with me.

"You won't get away. None of you will get away. Stop!"

'None of you will get away.' What did that mean? Who said that? How many of us did he have kept as prisoners? I seemed to run slower when I thought. I decided that better not think, all I had to do was escape.

I crossed the road. I was in luck. There was lots of space, but then the lights changed, and he couldn't follow me. I couldn't hear him over the traffic either. It was very comforting, but I had to keep going. Oh dear. A car honked its horn as he dived out in front of it. I was tired. He was gaining on me. Oh, bugger! He'd grabbed my hair and pulled me backwards. I saw a flash of metal; a long, sharp blade. He held it to my neck and sliced me, but my captor reached out.

"Oh no you don't! Not that one. You leave her be."

My attacker dropped me backwards onto the ground. That made my knees burn and my head hit the pavement. My neck was bleeding. I felt so dizzy, and blood dripped onto my hand.

My captor grabbed him and beat him until he moved away from me. My attacker ran. As he made his escape, I smiled at my captor who had come to my rescue.

"I won't let you die," he said. "I'll look after you, I always have."

I think it must have been then that I passed out because I don't remember anything after that.

Chapter Forty-Seven

"Why do you want to know if I was adopted?" Craig asked Angus. "I mean, it's a bit of a strange question, isn't it? Whether I'm adopted or not doesn't make me a better person or even a better butcher." He sipped his tea and frowned.

"It's important to our investigations," Angus said.

"Well, I never was. My big brother Donny and I were taken into care when I was only tiny. Three or four, I was. Apparently, our parents were a waste of space, and we were removed for our own good. They must have been shite because the care system's no great shakes. We were fostered together at first, but later we got split up and I was in and out of foster homes and children's homes. I haven't seen Donny in years."

"Do you have a sister?" Angus asked.

"I vaguely remember another child, Jane I think her name was, but I couldn't tell you for sure. Donny's the only one I remember clearly because he was with me for a while and looked out for me."

"Would you mind giving us a sample of your DNA?"

"I suppose not. Why?"

"We're investigating a series of murders and the abduction of a police officer. Your DNA might help to eliminate you," Angus said. The bluntness of his answer drew an explosive response from Craig.

"And you think that was me? What just because I work in old man Wilson's butcher's shop and can chop up a cow really quick, I must be a murderer. Is that what you think? I don't bloody think so, pal. Am I free to go?"

"Of course you are, Craig," Tim said quietly. "Any time."

"Then I'm off. And your tea's rubbish." He stood up and

glowered at Angus.

"My colleague didn't mean to offend you," Tim said. "It's just that we have evidence that you may be closely related to the perpetrator of at least some of the crimes we have outstanding, and it would greatly assist us if you would voluntarily allow us to take your DNA because that could confirm our suspicions and eliminate you from these cases. Of course, as you are here voluntarily and helping us with enquiries, you are under no obligation."

"Hmm, I see." Craig hovered around his chair and then sat down again. "Well, how do you think I can help?"

"Perhaps you can tell us a bit about yourself. How long have you been a butcher?" Tim asked.

"The Wilsons were my last foster home. There aren't many who'll take in a teenage boy. I thought I'd be stuck in the care home until I was sixteen, but the Wilsons took me in. I was never any great shakes at school, so old Robert took me on in the shop. He said it would keep me out of trouble. So, he'd get me up at five in the morning, for porridge and a bacon roll and we'd be in the shop for six, cleaning, chopping, slicing and preparing for opening at nine." Craig laughed and shook his head. "I was so bloody tired by the end of the day. I didn't have to energy to go looking for trouble. So, I suppose his plan worked."

"Do you still live with them, the Wilsons?" Tim asked.

"No, I live with my girlfriend, Julie, in Gorgie. We're wanting to get engaged soon."

"Congratulations. Does Mr Wilson still work in the shop?"

"He says he's retired, but he'll come in if we're overly busy, or if it comes up his back to see we're doing things right. He still owns the business and managed to get in the picture when I won that trophy a few weeks back. They're good people, the Wilsons."

"Do you have kids?" Tim asked.

Craig's eyes filled with tears. "We had two, a boy and a girl, but our wee lassie died last year. An accident they said it was. It didn't feel like an accident; it was a hit and run. They say we're young and can have another one. How would you feel

181

about that? Like she can just be replaced." He stared at Tim. "It's not like getting a new television or that. She was a person. She was our wee one and a light went out the day she died. That's why Julie always lights a candle in the window, so she can find her way. It's awful thinking of her being out there alone."

The butcher wiped his eyes with his sleeve and sniffed. He accepted the tissue Tim offered him and blew his nose loudly. He stuck the soggy tissue in his pocket and began to speak again.

"Anyway, that's not what you want to hear. What do you want from me?"

"How old was your daughter when she died?" Angus asked.

"Only four."

"Four, are you sure?"

Craig turned an unhealthy shade of red. "Are you for real?" he shouted. Do you believe there is any way on God's green earth I would forget or mis-speak about my kid's age when that fucking moron killed her? He came around that corner far too bloody fast and the wee one had no chance."

"I'm sorry, Mr Smith, I didn't mean that the way it sounded. Of course, you're not going to make a mistake about your children."

"I need a fag."

Tim adjourned the interview and Neil escorted Craig out to the car park. They both lit up and stood in silence, alternating their attention between the gravel underfoot and the cloudy sky up above.

***

By the time Craig came back in, he was calmer.

Tim recommenced the interview by asking if he would like another cup of tea.

"Aye, go on."

"Neil do the honours, please."

"Your wish is my command."

"So, Mr Smith. I suppose you must have been working at

Robert Wilson's shop for several years," Tim said.

"Aye, over ten years now."

"I believe it is one of the most highly thought of butchers in the city."

"You would think that if you listen to old man Wilson. But aye, it's been there a long time, so he must have been doing something right."

"And he has some well-known names amongst his customers, doesn't he?"

"He does that. Her that wrote all those wizard books, the First Minister, and he even supplies Holyrood Palace if they're having a do."

"My goodness, that's quite a responsibility," Angus said.

"It is. Do any other famous people shop there, for example, Lady Munro?" Tim asked.

"Yep. Several of the judges buy their meat there. They usually call an order in and get it delivered, but since she lived on her own, Lady Munro used to come in and get her meat. Just a wee drop compared to when the family were together. Shame about the old dear."

"You heard?"

"Her son phoned. Incredibly sad."

There was a silence and then Craig giggled.

"What's funny?"

"Someone told me she was on a dating site, and it was a sex thingy gone wrong."

"Who said that?" Angus asked.

"I don't remember."

"Convenient," said Tim. "However it happens, murder isn't funny."

"She deserved it, gave that driver far too short a sentence for killing my wee girl." He looked angry again and breathed deeply before he changed the subject. "We provide meat for Dolores Cline, the designer. Did you know she dresses royalty? And that poet, what's her name? Anyway, she's Mrs Dalgleish. She's quite famous for a poet."

"She's also dead," Tim said.

"As is Dolores Cline," Angus said.

"I know, but that's not my fault."

"Isn't it?" Tim asked. "You're pretty upset about the way Lady Munro dealt with the driver who ran over your daughter. You even found her death funny."

"Nah, I'm nervous, that's all."

"You didn't seem too upset about Ms Cline, or Mrs Dalgleish's death either."

"They're only customers, aren't they? I don't really care. It's a shame and all, but it's not as if I know them like friends."

"Nice," Tim said. "I think we're going to want another word with you, Mr Smith. Book him in, Neil," Angus said.

"What? What's going on?"

"I'm arresting you on suspicion of murder."

"This isn't funny."

"Murder rarely is."

Chapter Forty-Eight

Amar and Judy arrived at the address Mel had given them.

"Fuck! It's a tenement," Amar said.

"Well, what did you think 2f1 meant?" Judy asked.

"I didn't read that bit. I suppose it's second floor, first door."

"Well done. Are you sure your brother is the brains of your family? You're really quick?"

"Don't be so bloody sarcastic. Do we have any back-up?"

"Not that I know of. Now, shall we go and see if it's Donald Smith's flat? I don't think asking the guy's name warrants back-up," Judy said.

"But if we hear Jane calling out and have to barge in, it might."

"Shall we stay in the car and bicker or get on with our job?"

Amar opened his door and led the way from the car to the tall grey building. "It's not a fancy area, is it?"

"I can't say I expected a squaddie to have a grand house. He's doing well to have bought a flat."

"Half of me hopes we hear Jane, and the other half hopes we don't."

"What do you mean, Amar? Surely you want to find her?"

"Yes, I just don't like confrontation."

"Then I think you're in the wrong job. Come on, follow me." Judy raced up the stairs ahead of him.

She reached the second floor and paused. "Second floor, first door, wasn't it?"

"That's right," Amar said. He arrived just behind her. "The door's open." He glanced at her and pushed the door wider. "I think I heard somebody call out."

"I didn't."

He winked at her. "Are you sure you didn't hear someone call for help."

"Maybe I did. We better go and check."

Amar walked into the flat, calling out to anybody who might be there. He noticed every room was clean, neat, and tidy, except for the boxroom. A chair lay on its side and the bed was unmade. There was a rope of plastic bags tied together across the floor, the vinyl was sticky underfoot and the room smelt dreadful. One lightbulb glowed dimly in the centre of the room. He realised where the smell was coming from when he noticed the large bucket in the corner. It stank of disinfectant and piss. Amar boaked.

"I think I've found where someone was held. Possibly Jane."

Judy followed him into the windowless prison. "God, it's fucking honking in here. Poor Jane."

"Or whoever. We don't know it was Jane," Amar retched again. "I've got to get out of here. It's stinking."

"But only this boxroom because of the bucket. The rest of the place is well kept. Let's have a look and see if we can find anything to identify the owner," Judy said.

She walked into the living room and pulled open the top drawer of the sideboard. It was full of documents. Bingo.

"Amar, I've got him. Bank statements, wage slips and credit card statements all in the name of Donald Smith."

"Good, but no sign of him, or Jane or anybody else. We never seem to catch a break, do we?"

"Let's call the boss."

Chapter Forty-Nine

I remember I felt dizzy before I passed out. My head was aching, and I could see my captor's boots beside my head. I moved my arms up to protect myself in case he kicked me.

"I'm not going to hurt you. I never have, have I?"

I tried to shake my head, but the pavement got in the way.

He crouched down beside me. I saw tattoos on his legs. It was him, my stalker. What did he ever want with me? He spoke softly.

"I've called the ambulance, but I won't wait with you. It'll be too much trouble explaining everything. Just tell them I kept you safe from the killer, will you?"

I tried to nod, but my brain felt like it was going to explode.

"Here they come. I'm off. I've got to get back to barracks. There's your phone. I've switched it on. Stay safe, Janey."

I wondered what had happened to my phone. I tried to ask him, again, how he knew my name, but the words didn't come before he was gone. I think it was then I realised who my captor was, just before I lost consciousness.

***

There was excitement in the incident room at Gartcosh. Brian ran through to speak to DI Jallow.

"Boss, I've just had a call from communications. Jane's phone is back on. They say it's her work number, not her personal one, but it doesn't matter, they've traced her, and can track her, because she's on the move."

"Brilliant news, Brian. Where is she?"

"They told me she's moving across the south of Edinburgh towards the suburbs. The speed suggests she's in a car."

"Judy and Amar are in the city. Get hold of them and tell them to contact communications and get the details so they can follow Jane."

Jallow's phone rang. She lifted the handset swiftly. "This better be important," she growled.

"It is, boss. I think we've found where Jane was held. We've certainly found Donald Smith's flat."

"Fantastic, Judy. I'll call the local boys and CSIs. In the meantime, Jane's phone is back on. She's in a car heading from the south of the city towards the outskirts. You and Amar get going, and I'll have communications call you to fix you onto her route."

"Yes, boss. The door of the flat was open."

"Never mind the fucking flat. That's no longer your responsibility. The CSIs will deal with it. You find Jane."

***

"I don't care what Jallow says. We don't know the city and we don't know where she's being taken. Let's wait until communications contact us and give us information we can use."

Amar's phone rang. He listened while the communications expert gave him the information he needed. He thanked them and ended the call.

"The car she's in has stopped. She's at the Royal Infirmary of Edinburgh. It's in a place called Little France. Can you find it on Google Maps, while I drive?"

"Of course. Let's go," Judy said. "Come on, man. Drive!"

Chapter Fifty

It was a bugger that I'd messed up that attack on the policewoman. Donald was an idiot taking her to his own flat. Did he think that would protect her? Did he think I didn't know where his place is? I know them all, who they are, what they do, where they live. I know all about each of them.

Of course, it's clear I'm the brains of the family. A squaddie, a butcher a copper and me. I'm the smart one.

I had to run away from the copper. I didn't get a good enough swipe at her, she might survive. I ran as far as I could and then I saw a taxi and jumped into it, that got me to Waverley Station, and away from the scene. From there, I could get a train back to Glasgow. It was still early enough that I'd be back in time for classes. I never miss a lecture am never late and my flatmate thought I was at the library when I wasn't at home. It was none of his business.

At one point I thought it would be good to drive to and fro between the big cities, but parking in Edinburgh is impossible, not that it's much better in Glasgow, so I worked out that train travel would be best. Of course, I always pay cash for my tickets. Nobody could ever prove where I had been or when. Oh yes, there are cameras in the station and on the trains, but if nobody knows to look there, nobody is going to find me. I am a busy medical student who is always quiet, always studying, always has my nose in a book and hardly ever in Edinburgh.

When I saw the one with the green flash in her hair through the window of the train, I thought I was getting a second chance at her, but I missed the damn train. By only a few seconds, but I did.

She was sitting by a window, staring out down the platform, the freak with the green hair, sitting on the train to Glasgow.

Where was she going so early? I had spotted her, just before it left. I ran. I would have jumped onto any carriage, but I was just too slow, and the train left without me. I wondered if she was going all the way to Glasgow. Not that it really mattered, because she was on the train, and I wasn't. It's not as if I'd catch up with her. I wouldn't know where to look. Fuck! I missed my chance, again. The fates must be looking out for her. Pity about her colleague at the university. He wasn't so lucky. I hope he enjoyed working with her because it was her fault he died. He died for no reason except being in the wrong place at the wrong time. And because he saw my face, he had to go.

Then, miracle of miracles, I saw her in the canteen, but she saw me. I thought I saw recognition in her eyes, probably from the train station. I can follow her out, thank God. I'll get rid of her this time. But no, I can't. Damn and blast, she's with one of the staff. It's too dangerous for me. Someone might see me. I'll have to let her go, again but I'll get her. I'll make sure of that. I'll get them all.

I've done so well. I can't mess it up just for her. Only when I've got them all will justice be done, because my girl was worth more than all of them put together.

I didn't even know about her for the first year of her life, until I caught up with Kim again at that rugby match in Edinburgh. And it wasn't her who told me, it was her mad friend whose name I can never remember, Babs, maybe?

But my little girl was wonderful. Beautiful and funny and clever and kind. The most amazing child I had ever met. Like me, she was clever, very clever. Kim never allowed me to tell her I was her dad. That was harsh.

But you know what was even worse? She died in the fucking dentist's chair. Kim can't have cleaned her teeth properly because she had to get them all taken out.

After all, how dare the one with the flash of green in her hair and those other fools on the jury find that dentist not guilty of murder? How could they say it was just negligence that killed my wee one? I am going to get every last one of them. Let them suffer. Let them feel the life blood run out of their bodies and know they face death. I like to watch them while they try to hold their necks to keep it in. That's very funny, and I need a good laugh. We *all* need a good laugh when we have suffered a tragedy in our lives.

Chapter Fifty-One

Mackay called the briefing to order. Nobody paid him any attention. Regina looked at him and he nodded at her. She thumped the desk in front of him with a folder and called for quiet. Silence split the air.

"Right, can we have a bit of quiet? DI Jallow will update us on progress. Regina, go ahead," Mackay said.

Jallow nodded. "We have made significant progress on the murders and the abduction of DS Renwick."

"Have we found Jane, boss?" Brian asked.

"No, but we know where she is. Or we think we do because her work phone has been switched on again. It was moving, but it's stopped outside the Edinburgh Royal Infirmary. Amar and Judy are on their way now. I'm just waiting to hear from them."

"What about the murders?" Mackay asked.

"Angus and a local DC, Tim Myerscough, have identified the killer. He has been charged and is being held in Fettes Police Station in Edinburgh.

"Excellent news. Myerscough is sound. I'll tell the superintendent. Which brother is the killer?"

"Craig, Craig Smith the middle brother."

"He's a butcher or something, isn't he?" Brian asked.

"Yes, he won a competition for dissecting a cow recently."

"I suppose as a butcher he would know how and where to slice animals and, by extension, people," Mackay mused.

"Well, all the brothers would. One is a soldier, so he's trained to kill, and the youngest is a medical student. He'd have to know about the vital areas of the body so he could save people, but, presumably, he would also know how to kill them." Brian looked down to his desk and shook his head.

"I'm glad we've got him though. That man is a butcher right enough."

Regina's phone rang. "I need to take this, sir, it's Amar."

"Yes, yes go ahead. Put him on speaker so we can all hear."

"Hello, boss. We've found Jane. She was in the back of an ambulance. Her neck has been sliced, just like the murder victims, but she's still alive. They've taken her straight into surgery."

"Oh God. Right, how did she look, Amar?"

"Bloody, white as a sheet. Bad, boss. She looked terrible. But one of the A & E doctors seemed to know her, Ailsa Myerscough."

"That's not a common name, and it's the same name as the local DC who's working with Angus."

"Ailsa is Tim's sister. She's a medic in A & E at the Royal Infirmary, moved up from London a few years ago. Very able," Mackay said.

"She's not doing the surgery. Apparently Jane is a good friend, so she's got one of her specialist colleagues to do the op."

"I don't think an A & E medic would do that surgery anyway," Mackay said.

"Well, she's not. We can't find out who called the ambulance, though."

"It's not going to be the attacker, is it? We'll need to trace the number back from the call centre," Regina said. "But look, you said Jane's injuries were just like the murder victims'?"

"Yes, boss. Almost identical. Just not as deep. Jane probably wriggled, and the attacker couldn't get exactly the right angle or force that he wanted."

"Also, it must be a new knife because didn't he drop one when he sliced that Edinburgh DC," Regina said.

"Still, the second, signature cut down the breastbone is there. We've never made that public, have we, boss?"

"No, we held that back. Nobody but the killer would know about that. Bugger."

"What's the matter?"

"That means we have charged the wrong man with the

murders." The DI looked at Mackay.

"Fuck." He scowled back at her. "Just as well I haven't said anything to the super then. I better contact Angus and tell him the news."

***

Tim and Angus were just about to reward themselves with a coffee in the canteen when PC Neil Larken shouted to Angus, "Hey mate, it's your boss on the phone for you. She sounds really pissed off."

"Why? We've just caught her bloody killer."

"She's pissed off because apparently you've charged the wrong man, you numpty."

Angus was followed by Tim as he ran to take the call. He was out of breath when he spoke. "Neil said we've charged the wrong man."

"He's right."

"What do you mean, boss? Craig is Jane's brother. He's a butcher who knows how to slice up bodies. He lives in Edinburgh and knows all our victims. He admitted to knowing all of them, except the university guy."

"That may be true, but have you taken fingerprints and compared them to the ones we've found at the murder sites?"

"Well, we've taken his prints, but they've not been run through the system yet."

"What about his DNA? Have you compared that to the database?"

"I'm waiting to get that report back. How do you know it's the wrong guy?"

"I don't *know,* but I think it's unlikely that he's our man."

"How come?"

"We've found Jane."

"That's great news, boss."

"It is, but she's been gravely injured in an almost identical way to our murder victims. It seems she was attacked outside and moved enough that her assailant didn't manage to slice her neck as deeply as the others."

"She survived then, did she?"

"She's alive, but severely hurt. She's being operated on at the Royal Infirmary of Edinburgh."

"Oh no. What do I tell Rachael? I hope she pulls through."

"Me too, Angus. I'll get Amar to pick you up on his way back to Gartcosh. Is DC Myerscough with you just now?"

"Yes, he's right here. I'll put him on, boss."

"DC Tim Myerscough, ma'am," said Tim.

"DC Myerscough, I've been informed that your sister is a doctor in accident and emergency at the Royal Infirmary in Edinburgh."

"Yes, ma'am. She's a registrar."

"She was the attending medic when Jane was taken in," Jallow said.

"It's great we've got Jane. Good job by your team."

"No, by the time they got to the address we think she was held, the place was empty. However, we found Jane because someone turned her phone back on and Amar and Judy followed her to the hospital. I hear your sister recognised her and got her to the right surgical experts pronto."

"Ailsa knows Jane and Rachael well. Of course she would recognise her. Is Jane going to be all right?"

"I don't know yet. Keep in touch with the hospital and let me know, will you Myerscough?"

"Yes, ma'am."

"And release that fucking butcher." Regina hung up and turned to Mackay. "So what do we do now, sir?"

"Get Amar and Judy back from Edinburgh and let's look again at what we've got. Has the DNA from the youngest brother been processed yet?"

"Let me check. Want a coffee, sir?"

"No, I want a double whisky, but I suppose a coffee will have to do."

Chapter Fifty-Two

"Brian, do we have the home address for Troy Bean?" Regina asked.

"Yes, boss, I'm sure we do. He gave it to Angus and Amar when they met with him. It's out near Glasgow University, because he's only a student, if I recall correctly. Amar said he's a nice guy. He was very co-operative, and he knows Amar's brother."

"Enough chat. Just get it for me, will you?"

Regina wandered back into her office and closed the door. She leaned on the wooden frame and closed her eyes. The youngest brother might be as personable as Amar thought, but it didn't mean he wasn't a killer. A medical student would know just where to slice a body to make it count. Or the older brother, he was a soldier. He would know too. Soldiers were trained to kill, weren't they? But why would either of them do that? She closed her eyes. Motive, what was their motive? Every killer had a reason for carrying out a murder, what was it here? She opened her eyes, walked slowly towards her desk, and sat down. Mackay was right, whisky would have tasted much better than this coffee right now.

***

As soon as Tim finished speaking to Regina, Angus brought him up to date on all he knew.

"So, we've to let the butcher go?" Tim asked. "Let's release him on bail, just in case."

"Let's do that. Amar and Judy are going to swing by and pick me up. I'm to go back to Gartcosh."

"I'll phone Rachael and tell her about Jane and then I'm

going over to the hospital. I've to keep DI Jallow up to date with Jane's progress," Tim said.

"I don't envy you that call to Rache. It's a bugger Jane was so badly injured."

"But good she survived."

Tim's conversation with Rachael was extremely short. He had no sooner told her where Jane was when she replied, "Thanks, Tim. I'm on my way." She hung up. Tim tried to phone back to offer to drive her to the hospital, but the line was already engaged. He guessed she was calling a cab. She wouldn't be thinking straight.

He dialled Gillian and she picked up right away.

"Hello, lovely lady. How did your talk go?"

"Well thanks, pet. How has your day been?"

Tim told her about Jane.

"Thank God she's alive," she said. "The train's just pulling into Waverley Station now. Do you want me to head over to the hospital and keep you company?"

"You don't have to do that, Gillian. It won't be any fun."

"I know I don't have to, but I'd like to be there for you. I'll grab a cab from the station and be with you as soon as I can."

"Thanks. I'll try to contact Rachael offer to drive her over. I'll meet you there."

***

Neil Larkin was at reception. "Rachael? No, you've just missed her, Tim. I don't know where she's gone but she fair flew out of here."

Tim told Neil about Jane.

"No wonder Rache was in a hurry. You off to the hospital too?"

"Yes. I've to keep the DI in Gartcosh in the loop."

"Give the girls my best, won't you? Is Angus going back to the wild west?"

"Yes. Angus is getting picked up to go back to MIT, and I'll tell Rachael you're asking after them. Now, I must go."

***

The first person Tim saw at the hospital was Ailsa. "How is she?" he asked without introduction.

"Oh, Tim, it's a nasty injury. She's lucky it wasn't any deeper or she'd have bled out in just a couple of minutes."

"Thank goodness it was no worse. Do you think she'll pull through?"

"I hope so. I called in the lead consultant surgeon. I couldn't have done the op. I know Jane far too well."

"Of course. Well, she's in the best hands."

"She truly is."

"Have you seen Rachael, sis?"

"Yes, she's sitting in the waiting room. I've spoken to her, but she's as white as a sheet. She almost looks as bad as Jane did."

"No big surprise there. I'll go and join her. If you see Gillian, will you tell her where we are?"

"What do you think I am? The greeter at Asda? I've got a department full of patients to treat. If you want Gillian to know where you are, text her." Ailsa strode off into A & E leaving Tim speechless.

He sent the suggested text to Gillian and went in search of Rachael.

Chapter Fifty-Three

"I fully expect to be promoted to detective by the end of the day," Neil said to Angus.

"How do you work that out?"

"You're the third detective to leave here in half an hour. There's bound to be a shortage before the day is out."

"Can I just remind you that I don't actually work here?"

"That's the most honest thing I've heard a detective say, ever." Neil grinned.

"Fuck off."

Angus saw Amar pull up in the car. He opened the door and went over. He told them about the butcher and how he'd had to release him on bail while he got in.

"So, do you think it's the soldier or the young medic who's our killer?" Judy asked.

"It can't be the medic. My brother knows him."

"It can't be somebody your brother knows. That's nonsense."

"No, that's not what I mean, but he says that guy's top of his year and always studying. He's never without his nose in a book. And he won that surgery medal, you don't get that by bunking off," Amar said. "So, it can't be him, that's what I'm saying."

"And to be honest, he seemed like a decent guy," Angus added. "I mean, we both met him, and he was horrified that any blood relative of his could be a killer. He was happy enough to give us DNA and all that. I doubt it's him too."

"Also, he lives in Glasgow. Hardly the most convenient place for an Edinburgh serial killer to be," Judy agreed.

"Yeh, must be the soldier. When we got to his flat the door was open and there was nobody home," Amar said.

"But there was a stinking bucket in the boxroom. No window

in there but the pail had been used as a toilet," Judy said. She screwed up her nose as she remembered the smell. "Somebody had been kept in that wee room. Yuck. It was really pongy."

"I don't suppose we know it was Jane, but how many people are abducted and held at any one time?" Angus queried.

"I don't know that, but it was her brother's flat, so I'd bet money it was Jane. I just don't know how she got out," Amar said.

"I hope she lives long enough to tell us," Judy said.

They drove the rest of the way in silence, each wrapped in their own thoughts, each hoping against hope that Jane would pull through.

***

Angus knocked on DI Jallow's door. "That's us back, boss," he said.

"Good. Angus, have you got the DNA back from the youngest brother yet?"

"It should be through by now, boss, but I don't know if it's been checked. Anyway, Amar and Judy and I were just saying that it can't be the student. He lives in Glasgow and spends all his time studying. We assume it must be the soldier brother."

"You know what assume does, Angus?"

"Yes, boss, it makes an ass of you and me."

"Do I look like an ass to you?"

"No, boss."

"Check the student's DNA and let me know what you find."

"Yes, boss."

Angus walked back to report his new task to Amar and Judy.

"What fucking waste of time," Amar said.

"What did you say DC Patel?" Jallow said as she walked up behind the group.

"I said, what a good idea, why didn't I think of that, boss."

"That's what I thought. We're out of biscuits, and I need a sugar hit. It's your turn to get them, Amar."

He got up to go out and heard her shout after him. "Make sure they're chocolate."

200

Chapter Fifty-Four

I don't remember waking from the anaesthetic, but I do remember the dreams that followed the operation. They were not good dreams, but those that took me back to my childhood and through my life. It was all jumbled up.

They took me back to the earliest times I could remember shoplifting food to survive. Donny and I had to hide what we got from my parents, or they would steal it when they got the munchies.

Suddenly I was choosing my outfit for my civil partnership to Rachael. I was in the shop; it was warm there and Mel was with us. So much to choose from. How could I decide? Then we were drinking wine at a dinner party. I couldn't work out where we were before the picture changed again.

I was sitting exams at high school. Was I the only one who had done no revision? I didn't know any of the answers, hell, I didn't even understand the questions, never mind know the answers. How could this have happened? I always studied hard, but not this time, it would seem. And I had to keep leaving the room to change Craig's nappies. How much crap could a little boy have inside him? Why was I responsible for him? I was only a child too.

Next, I was riding my motorcycle, fast. Faster and faster, I sped through the narrow roads in the Scottish mountains and glens. Such beautiful scenery, but I couldn't see it properly. I was travelling too quickly to focus on that, just the winding road ahead of me. I felt my wheels wobble and I was falling; I couldn't catch myself.

Then Dad was on top of me. It hurt so much, even though I felt myself fall, I couldn't get away from him. I heard Donny; he was crying. So was I. Craig was sleeping. I could feel tears running down my cheeks. I woke when Rachael's fingers brushed them away. I heard her voice.

"Darling Janey, please don't cry. You're alive, and that's all that matters. Everything else we can sort. We'll work it all out together. You know that we always do."

I must have lost consciousness again because I was back at our union when her dad gave us both away. I saw her sister, Sarah, and Mel as our bridesmaids and Tim and Bear were our best men. Such a wonderful day.

But I wasn't there for long before I was locked in a small, smelly boxroom eating sandwiches and savouring chocolate. Chocolate, the day I was taken from my parents and the social worker took me down the stairs. She gave me chocolate. I never saw Donny or Craig again.

Then my captor whispered in my ear. 'I won't hurt you. I never have."

Donny used to say that when he pretended to slap me. People would give me money to make me feel better. They'd each just give me a little, but it all added up when he pretended to hit me, and I pretended to feel the pain. Then we could go a buy something from the shop instead of stealing it.

Donny was my captor!

Donny was the tattooed man!

Donny was my stalker!

Why?

Then I heard Rachael again.

"No, Tim, I don't want a fucking cup of tea. That will not help one bit. I want Janey to wake up and smile and for everything to be all right again. Oh, Tim. Look, her eyelashes are fluttering again. Get the doctor. I think she's waking up. Janey? Janey pet? Stay with me." She squeezed my hand. "Are you still here? Get a bloody doctor, Tim."

Chapter Fifty-Five

Brian stared at the confirmation from the forensics lab in disbelief. The lab had told him the report was already with them. He hadn't seen it. 'Well go and look for it,' they told him and hung up. Bloody hell, they were right enough. It had been sitting on Angus's desk for two days, but nobody had thought to look at it because Angus was in Edinburgh, and it was his desk. This information should have gone to DI Jallow or even DCI Mackay in his absence, but nobody thought. He didn't think. How could he make this Amar or Judy's fault? He didn't want to carry the can.

"What have you got there?" Jallow asked. She snatched the report out of his hand. "Good God!" she shouted. "How long have we had this? It's dated Tuesday. It's now Thursday. Where was it?"

Brian blushed furiously. "I found it there, on Angus's desk."

"But Angus was in bloody Edinburgh. Who put it there and why didn't they bring it to me?"

"It must have been Amar or Judy, boss. I've never seen it."

"Of course, you haven't. And even if you had you'd blame someone else."

"That's not fair, boss," he whined.

Jallow glared at him and marched through to give DCI Mackay the news.

***

Jallow could not remember a time when she'd seen Mackay look so angry. He read the report and then echoed the very sentiments she had uttered only moments before. Neither of them could fathom why this vital evidence had been ignored for so long. Eventually, Mackay sighed and began to cool down a bit. He took a long swig of coffee and pulled a face. It was cold and the milk was beginning to curdle on the top.

"Okay, Regina, let's get this done. I want a warrant to search that man's home. See it gets issued immediately, if not sooner."

"Yes, sir. I'll get right on it."

"Are McKenzie, Marsh and Patel back yet?"

"Yes, sir. They're not long back."

"Tell them to get them over to Glasgow University. I want them to track down Jane's student brother. Angus and Amar met him the first time, didn't they?"

"Yes, boss. They thought he was a good guy."

"Shows what fine judges of character they are, doesn't it?" Mackay said. "Well, if they can take him home and charm him into letting them in, they will be there when we get our warrant, and they can start the search right away."

"Yes, boss. Do you want Judy to go with them?" Regina asked.

"Yes. An extra pair of hands won't go amiss. Anything else?"

"Brian is still here. If I can get the warrant swiftly, he can take it over. We have the man's address."

"Fine. That's a good idea." Mackay paused and looked across his desk at Jallow. "The one thing I don't understand is why. What's the motive for a young Glasgow Medical Student to kill four members of Edinburgh society?"

"I don't know." Jallow shook her head. "It makes no sense to me, but the DNA and fingerprints are damning evidence."

She stood up and walked through to the incident room to give the orders, then went back to her own office to get preparation of the warrant started.

***

Angus felt his phone vibrate in his pocket. He wriggled in his seat to get at it.

"Ooh, DC McKenzie's vibrator, is it?" Judy teased.

"Shut up. No, sorry, not you, boss. Judy's being an arse." Angus grimaced at Judy. "What can I do for you?"

Angus listened in silence as Regina told him about further details in the forensics report. He tried to interrupt her to explain he hadn't known it was there, but the DI was in full flow. He didn't need to be looking at her to realise how angry she was, and her voice got louder and louder as she ranted about the time they had lost because of the oversight of the information. She wasn't on speakerphone, but Amar and Judy could hear every word she said as she bellowed into Angus's ear.

Finally she paused for breath. Angus surmised that she had run out of oxygen but decided not to offer a comment.

"Have you got nothing to say for yourself, DC McKenzie? It will take time to get the warrant, I need you and Patel to use your powers of persuasion on the suspect and get into his home."

"Yes, boss. Amar can be charming."

"Not so much of the lip, McKenzie. You lot just get this done, no more slip-ups. You're not the Marx brothers, you know."

"Of course, boss. We'll do our best."

"I need success, not your best, that hasn't been up to much recently, from any of you."

The others can't hear you, boss. You're not on loudspeaker."

"They can bloody hear me, McKenzie, and there will be a full investigation as to how the important report fell through the cracks and was ignored for over thirty-six hours. And I will bloody scalp all the culprits I uncover. Do you hear that?"

"Yes, boss." Angus noticed the DI had paused again, and thought he'd take a chance to be positive. "At least there were no more murders, boss."

"Is that meant to be funny?"

"Not at all."

"You three, I want you round to Glasgow University to talk to the medic again. The fingerprints and DNA identify him as having been at the scene of at least three of the murders. There

205

was nothing useful found at Dolores Cline's salon."

"Glasgow University. We're on our way now, boss."

Angus watched as Amar set the sat-nav for the quickest route to destination. He realised his colleague was taking no chances of getting this wrong.

"It's just that, I really can't see that it could be him, boss. I mean, he seems to be studying so much of the time. He seems to do nothing but study. I really can't see what interest he would have in these Edinburgh types. He said he's hardly ever in Edinburgh."

"Well, he would say that, wouldn't he? Anyway, this is not up for discussion. See if you can get him to accept a lift back to his flat and hopefully it won't be long after that that the warrant will be available. Brian'll bring it over."

"How will we get into the flat if the warrant isn't available? It'll look a bit odd if we just sit in the car outside."

"Oh, for goodness' sake, Angus. Use your initiative. One of the three of you must have some."

Regina rang off. Angus was delighted not to have her shouting in his ear any longer. He had never been aware of her being so angry but had heard rumours that she had a fearsome temper.

"Good call to tell her we couldn't hear her. Thanks for that," Amar said.

"I doubt that'll protect you for long, she's on the warpath."

"So, back to see Beanie, is it?"

"Yes, that DNA report was left on my desk and the fingerprints and DNA samples he gave us match those found at some of the murder scenes."

"Hmm, if I remember rightly, Angus, they didn't find anything useful at the first one, it was only after that the perpetrator got more and more careless."

"I think that's right, Judy."

"Back to the University canteen then. I'm bursting for a wee," Amar said.

"Thanks for sharing. I could go a coffee," Angus said.

"I want both," Judy said.

Chapter Fifty-Six

Jane stirred and Rachael grinned at Tim. "She's coming back to us," she whispered.

"Thank goodness. Look, Rache, I'll go and find Gillian, and we'll go for a coffee and leave you two together. We'll be back in about half an hour to see Jane, if that's all right with you."

"Thanks, Tim." Rachael gave him a quick kiss on the cheek and then turned her attention back to Jane.

Tim called Gillian and discovered she was already waiting in the café.

"I didn't want to intrude when you and Rachael were with Jane," she said when he went to join her.

"You wouldn't be intruding, pet. They're as much your friends as they are mine. Do you want anything to eat with that?" He pointed to her bottle of sparkling water.

"No thanks. I've already had a banana."

"I'm getting a coffee and the biggest slice of cake they have."

"Surprise, surprise."

When Tim sat back beside Gillian, she seemed extremely pensive.

"Penny for them?" he asked.

"I've been thinking. I've worked out where I know the names of the two women who were murdered."

"Dolores Cline and Beatrice Dalgleish? Or do you mean Lady Munro?"

"No, not her, everybody knows who Lady Munro is."

"I suppose so."

"But the other two that were murdered, they were on the jury with me, when that little girl died."

"Really? Are you sure?"

"Well, I remember the name Mrs Dalgleish, and there can't be that many people called Dolores living in Edinburgh."

"Wasn't Lady Munro the judge?"

"Yes, I was just getting to that." Gillian looked sad as she continued speaking. "What if there is a connection, Tim? What about if, the day that Zelay was killed, they were looking for me and killed him by mistake?"

"There's no way anybody could mistake you for Zelay."

"No, don't be silly. Hear me out. What if the murderer was wandering around the languages department late at night and asked Zelay where I was or something? Perhaps if he had seen their face, they felt they had to kill him to silence him. What if I'm the reason he's dead? Oh, God. I feel so guilty."

"Gillian, you are not guilty of anything. The person who killed Zelay and the other victims is an evil serial killer. You are not to blame for any of this."

"No of course you're right. Could I have a mint tea? It might help calm me down."

Tim went to the counter and bought a mint tea, another coffee and two KitKats. He thought Gillian could do with the sugar rush. He knew he needed one.

"Tell me about the case. Wasn't the victim a child from a one-parent family?"

"Yes, that's right. No father. The little one's milk teeth were completely rotten and had to be taken out."

"All of them?"

"Yes. The dentist didn't think the mother would bring the girl back, so he decided to do it there and then." Gillian looked sadly at Tim. "The girl was only three, Aqua Hourston her name was. Poor wee soul. She looked so scruffy in her photos and quite small, but a really pretty little girl."

"Aqua? That's a strange name."

"It is, yes. Apparently there was some sort of family fascination with the Stingray puppet show. I don't know. Anyway, the dentist miscalculated the child's weight by measuring it in kilos instead of pounds and she was given more than twice the anaesthetic that she would have needed. She died later in hospital. It was an incredibly sad case. The man was inconsolable."

"I imagine the kid's family was too."

"Of course. And when we found him not guilty of murder but of death due to his negligence, the family went crazy. We had to get the police to remove them because there were too many of them for court security to deal with."

"Gosh, that must have been frightening. I don't remember you saying anything at the time."

"I don't think we were allowed to. But yes, it was terrifying."

"It's most likely this killer is a man. Female serial killers are almost unknown. There have only been four convicted in the U.K. and none in Scotland that I know of. If you're right, maybe the murders we're seeing now were carried out by an uncle or a grandfather."

"I don't know. I just wondered if there was a connection that I should have made earlier and maybe saved Zelay."

"I can't see how you could have made that connection, pet. Let's face it, it's only with the benefit of hindsight that this occurred to you. By then, the victims were dead."

"You're probably right."

"I'm going to phone the DI in Gartcosh and tell her what we've been talking about, then let's go up and see Jane and Rachael." He smiled at her. "Are you going to eat that biscuit?"

"Yes, I jolly well am!"

Chapter Fifty-Seven

Amar drove as smoothly and swiftly as the traffic would allow, but the journey seemed to take forever. He, Angus, and Judy sat in silence. He could not understand how a man like Troy Bean could be involved in the atrocities of Edinburgh. He recalled the blood stains in Zelay's office, the post-mortems he had witnessed, and the conversations he had had with his brother. He thought Troy was a decent bloke too. Could they both really be so wrong?

He was so lost in his thoughts, he nearly missed the turn-off to the university and when he noticed it, he swung the car around the corner, jolting Angus and Judy about.

"Lucky we had our seatbelts on," Judy said.

"Too true. Now, how do we want to play this?" Angus asked Amar.

"I think let's go in softly, softly, tell him we've got new evidence that the DNA and fingerprints he volunteered were helpful, but don't indicate he's now our main suspect."

"What, three detectives just stopped by to say, 'Thanks very much?'" Judy sounded incredulous. "I thought this guy was meant to be intelligent."

"Well, what if you stay in the car, Judy and we go in to see him and say we were just passing and wanted to thank him for his help?" Angus said.

"Okay, and then we can offer him a lift home because we're going that way to get back to the station."

"Won't he notice me when he comes out to the car?"

"But then it'll be too late for him to refuse the lift without it looking odd," Amar said.

"Come on, let's go. The three of us sitting in the car in the carpark must look a bit odd too." Angus opened his door and began to walk towards the entrance.

"Hold up, Ginger. Wait for me."

Amar trotted to catch up with Angus, and they walked together towards the university building, along the corridor and into the canteen. Amar pulled the door open, and a waft of warm, coffee-scented air met them.

"You can't beat a good coffee," Angus said. "Except perhaps with a good whisky."

Amar smiled then looked around the canteen. "There he is, at the same table. I don't see how it can be him. He's got a laptop and a bundle of books. My brother says he's well known for being a swat."

"The forensics can't lie, though. Let's go over and speak to him," Angus said. "Beanie!" he called out when they were halfway across the room. "I'm glad we found you."

The student looked up. He seemed startled at first, but soon resumed his equilibrium and smiled.

"Hello, detectives. I don't suppose you can rise to another coffee for a poor student, can you?"

"Our pleasure. My shout today, I think," Amar said.

"And a muffin won't go amiss."

"Coming right up. You too, Angus?"

"Do you need to ask?" Angus grinned.

"To what do I owe this pleasure? Or did I park my bike in a mother and toddler bay at the supermarket?"

"You may have done, but if you did, it hasn't been reported."

"Thank goodness for that. So, do you need my help again? I'm training to be a doctor you know, not a detective."

Angus smiled. "Nothing like that."

He watched Amar weave his way back between the tables carrying a full tray.

"Well seen you're not a mathematician, you've got four of everything and we're only three," Troy said.

"She'd poured out the coffee, so I thought we'd take it back for our colleague rather than let it go to waste," Amar said. "Have you told Troy the good news?"

"No, I thought I'd wait till we were both here," Angus said.

"We were passing and thought we'd stop by to tell you that the DNA sample you gave us was extremely helpful. We've been able to arrest someone for those murders."

Was it just his imagination, or did Amar notice Troy seem uneasy? Then the student spoke, as if he hadn't a care in the world. "I heard on the news that they'd arrested a butcher in Edinburgh."

"Yes, that's right. I was involved in that arrest," Angus said.

"So it's someone who's related to me, is it?"

"Closely related. Maybe even a brother."

"That's awful, a butcher right enough," Troy stood up. "I'm really pleased I could help, but I've got to go. It's my turn to cook back at the flat tonight."

Angus and Amar stood too. "We'll give you a lift, we're going back that way."

"You don't know where I live," Troy said.

"You gave us your address the last time we met, remember?" Amar said.

"I did, didn't I? Well, a lift would be great, thanks."

This is all too easy, Amar thought. A medic must surely know that DNA would pin the evidence on one person. Does he have a plan? Is he playing us in some way? He led the way to the car and Angus followed on behind Troy.

When they got back to the car, Judy was standing outside. She had taken a chance to have a cigarette.

"I got you a decent coffee, Judy."

"Thanks, pal, but I can't drink it until I've made some space."

"Charming. This is Troy."

"Oh, the lad who helped us. These guys have been singing your praises all week. Especially since they arrested a suspect. Thanks for your co-operation."

Troy smiled. "Always happy to help the boys in blue, and the girls."

They all climbed into the car and Amar drove off down the road.

"What's parking like in your street?"

"You should get parked easily enough at this time of day."

It wasn't long till they pulled up near to Troy's apartment building.

"Thank for the lift, guys," he said as he got out of the back seat.

"Troy, would you mind if I came in and used your loo?" Judy asked. "I don't think I'll make it back to the station with my dignity intact, otherwise."

"And me?" Amar asked.

"Sure, that should be fine. I doubt my flatmate is even in. Just remember it's a lad's flat and it probably hasn't been cleaned in a month."

Judy wrinkled her nose. "Beggars can't be choosers."

Angus followed them towards the building.

"If you need to go too, I'll have to start charging," Troy joked.

'If you're guilty, you're one cool customer,' Amar thought.

"No, I'll just wait outside," Angus said. Then he felt his phone vibrate in his pocket. The text message was from DI Jallow.

Brian on his way with warrant. Ask TB if the name Aqua means anything to him and watch his response. We believe she was his daughter who died when a dentist made a mistake.

"Sure you don't want to come inside and wait?"

"Thanks, that's kind of you. I will." Angus followed the others into the hallway. "We think the butcher had a daughter who died. when a dentist made a mistake. She was only four, Aqua, her name was."

"She was three."

"What was that?" He watched Troy closely as Troy repeated himself.

"Three. Aqua was only three years old when that fucking dentist killed her."

"Read about it in the papers, did you?" Angus asked. He tried to string out the talk but wished Brian would get here pronto. Things could turn nasty, quickly if he wasn't careful.

Right on cue, the doorbell rang. Troy didn't reply to Angus's question. He went to open the door.

Angus was relieved to see Brian standing there surrounded

by a team of CSIs. He moved up the hall to introduce Brian, and then let his colleague explain the warrant.

"Why do you want to search here? He told me you'd arrested a butcher from Edinburgh."

"We did. He's been released on bail. Are you any relation to Kim Hourston?" Brian asked.

"No."

"Let me put it another way. Were you the father of Kim Hourston's daughter, Aqua Hourston, who died due to the negligence of her dentist last year?"

"Negligence? Are you really calling it negligence? It was murder, plain and simple." Troy started to wail. He slipped down the wall and held his head in his hands. "She was only three. Three years old. I'd only found out I had a daughter a year before that. Her fucking mother wasn't ever going to tell me, was she? Lucky she's got a friend with a big mouth."

Then Angus noticed Troy looked to the side. He stood up slowly but then gained speed as he rammed his way past Angus, moving swiftly towards the open kitchen window. He raced straight into Amar, winding him, but there was no way to get past Judy. She stuck her foot out and the student clattered to the ground. Angus couldn't help but laugh as Judy sat on top of the stunned man, explained his rights, and cuffed him.

"You okay, pal?" she asked Amar.

"I've been better. But thanks, Judy."

"What about you and Angus take this one to face the tender mercies of DI Jallow and I'll stay here with Brian to search the flat?"

"Fine by me," Amar said.

Chapter Fifty-Eight

Jane gazed around the room. She tried to focus. There seemed to be many people around her. The nurse held one arm to take her blood pressure while Rachael held her other hand and stared at the ceiling.

"Why are you crying, Rache?" Jane asked.

That was it, the flood gates opened, and tears poured down Rachael's cheeks.

"Because I was bloody scared that I'd lost you forever, and I don't know how to work the new vacuum cleaner." She tried to smile, but the expression was not a complete success.

"I've worked out who my stalker was."

"That's the least of our worries. He's gone."

"No, he hasn't, he's gone back to work."

"Your stalker has a job? Or is stalking his job?"

"He's a soldier. He's my brother Donny. He would never hurt me. He never has and he never will."

"Jane, I hate to state the obvious, but he abducted you. Took you and held you captive against your will," Tim said softly.

Jane took a moment to focus on the tall, blond man and then she smiled.

"Tim, how are you?"

"Silly. How are you, more to the point?"

"Jane, did you give evidence in that case where the little girl died because she got too much anaesthetic?"

"Who's that?" Jane squinted to get sight of Gillian. "Oh, hello. Yes, I did. I think I was the only officer called. The family wanted the young dentist to be charged with murder, but he got done for culpable homicide as a result of negligence. Shame about the wee girl, but there's no way it was murder."

Jane lifted her hand to her head. Then she ran her fingers across her neck. She felt the long scar and flinched.

"More pain relief?" the nurse asked.

"Please."

"I think we should call an end to visiting time."

"Can I stay, if I just sit quietly?" Rachael asked.

"Please let her," Jane said.

The nurse nodded and held the door open for Tim and Gillian to leave.

"If Jane's right, and she was one of the witnesses in that same case, the attack on her was probably connected with the murders."

"How awful. Imagine if she'd..."

"Don't say it. But I must call DI Jallow and tell her what Jane said."

***

Jallow and Amar sat across from Troy in the interview room. Troy had never been in a police interview room before. He looked around. How musty it was. The horrible smell made him gag. The tables and chairs were metal and bolted to the floor. Even the old ashtray was secured to the table, rather at odds with the *No Smoking* sign. There was a recording device and that was bolted on to the table and high on the wall was a camera. He stared at it and wondered if somebody could see him now. Probably not. If the lens was as thick with grease as the fixing holding it to the wall, they had no chance.

There was a policewoman by the door. Troy looked at her and thought in other circumstances he might have a shot at her. She was pretty and he knew he was no slouch. He moved around on his seat to see the wall behind him. The only window was there, but it was too high up to see out of and it had bars in front of it with big, thick cobwebs joining them up. This place was nasty.

The door opened and the red-haired detective and a short black woman walked in.

"Thanks for coming in to talk to us today, Troy," she said.

216

"I didn't have much of a choice," he said sourly.

"Probably not. We are talking to all the people who may be able to help us in a murder case."

"Would you like a cup of tea?" the red-headed one asked.

"I prefer coffee. White."

He watched the pretty constable leave the room and decided he would definitely have a shot at her.

The black woman introduced herself as Detective Inspector Jallow and re-introduced Detective Constable Angus McKenzie.

"I've met him before," Troy said.

DI Jallow nodded and explained they would be taping the discussion because of its importance, but that Troy was entitled to have a lawyer present if he wanted.

"Do I need one?" Troy asked.

"I can't answer that. If you want one, and have a lawyer, we can contact them for you. If you don't have one, I can have one appointed for you."

The younger woman came back into the room. Troy smiled, but noticed her expression didn't change. Probably not a good sign. She put Troy's coffee in front of him and he winked at her. She blushed. He was right, he could take her. He sipped his drink. He hated hot drinks out of plastic cups. He watched DI Jallow carefully. It was clear that she was in charge.

"Mr Bean, do you want to have a lawyer present?"

"Let's start without one and see how we get on. I can change my mind, can't I?"

"You can change your mind, but what has been said can't be unsaid."

"Crack on then." Troy smiled, then he raised his cup to the constable by the door.

Chapter Fifty-Nine

Tim and Gillian decided to go home. There was no benefit to either of them nor to Jane and Rachael if they stayed and waited at the hospital. They walked past Ailsa on the way out.

"How is she?" she asked.

"She's awake. A bit fussy headed and still in pain, but she's awake," Tim said.

"That's more than I'd expected, to be honest. You off home then?"

"Yes. When do you finish?" Gillian asked.

"An hour ago. I just want to see how another of my admissions is doing and then I'll follow you up the road."

"I was thinking of getting us a fish supper tonight. Do you want me to get one for you?"

"That would be fab, Tim. I know there will be some dinner left for me, there always is, but it will be overcooked and tasteless by the time I get back. I can just heat the fish supper in the microwave."

"No problem, sis. See you when you get home." Tim kissed Ailsa lightly on the cheek and followed Gillian out to the car park.

"I think you should phone the lead officer now, if you're going to," Gillian said.

"You're right. I almost forgot, lost in the truly important matter of fish suppers."

"Mine's a white pudding supper, please."

"Yes, dear. Oh, can I speak to DI Jallow, please?" Tim paused to listen. "Who's she with?" He pulled a face. "The thing is it might be my business. Hell, just tell her DC Tim Myerscough called from Fettes in Edinburgh about DS Jane Renwick. Yes, *that* Jane Renwick." Tim hung up. "What a fucking jobsworth."

He opened the car and they got in. They began the drive across the city to Morningside.

***

DI Jallow could cuss with the best of them, and she illustrated her ample vocabulary when, as she was just getting to the nub of the matter with Troy, there was a knock at the door and Amar popped his head in.

"Boss, reception has just taken a call for you. I think you may want to call back."

"You better be right, DC Patel. Interview suspended at 18.05."

"You want another coffee?" Angus asked Troy.

"Will it taste any better than the last one?"

"I doubt it."

"No thanks. Just a glass of water, please."

***

"This better be good, Myerscough. I came out of an interview with the murder suspect for this," Regina growled.

"I wouldn't call it good, but maybe relevant, ma'am."

"What's up? Are you driving? I hope you're on hands free."

"It's about Jane. Yes, and of course."

"Don't be a smart arse, Myerscough. Nobody likes a smart arse."

"True, ma'am."

"Well, spit it out, boy."

"My girlfriend and I went to see Jane Renwick."

"She's out of surgery?"

"She is. She's a bit groggy and still in pain, but she's conscious."

"Thank the Lord. What's the news?"

"Well, you recall Gillian remembered that she had been on a jury with Dolores Cline and Beatrice Dalgleish in a case heard by Lady Munro?"

219

"Yes, and she was eating herself up because she thought poor old Zelay Scheptytsky might have been murdered when the killer was on the hunt for her."

"Exactly, ma'am. Well, when we were talking to Jane, she said she was the only police officer to give evidence at that same trial. We wondered if Jane's attack…"

"Wasn't random?"

"Yes, and Jane seems to think that her abductor is her older brother, Donny. Donald Smith. He is the soldier Angus and I looked for but kept missing."

"And whose apartment was empty when Amar and Judy got to it. It's all beginning to fall into place. I'll go and speak to DCI Mackay and then I want to get back to Troy Bean and crack a nut."

"Sounds painful ma'am."

"Perhaps for him. But I won't feel a thing."

Chapter Sixty

"Now, where were we, Mr Bean?" Regina said as she re-entered the interview room. She congratulated herself on not grinning when she said his name.

"Somebody was going to bring me a glass of water."

"It's coming."

Angus walked in and placed the water in front of Troy. He noticed the man did not look as calm as he had done previously. His palms had left sweaty prints on the metal table. He and Regina had agreed that he would take over the questioning.

"Troy, who took Aqua to the dentist that day?"

"Kim told me she did. I really had nothing to do with her upbringing. Like I said, she hadn't been going to tell me the child was even mine. I didn't meet her until about a year before she died, on her second birthday. She didn't have my name, but Kim called her Aqua in a nod to me. That was nice of her, I suppose."

"When you learned about the wee one, did you ask for a DNA test?"

"Oh yes. I wasn't going to be taken for a mug."

"And she was your child?"

"Yes, the most amazing child in the universe."

"When did you learn about her death?"

"Kim told me that day. She phoned me. We hardly ever phoned, usually texted, but that day she phoned. Said the dentist killed her. He'd called an ambulance, but it was too late, she died. Too much anaesthetic, you see. She was only wee."

"That must have been awful."

"If you don't have kids, you won't know, but it felt like

somebody had ripped my heart out."

"Did you go to court?"

"I couldn't go every day, I had classes, and the case was heard in the High Court in Edinburgh. I went when I could. Kim and her family sat in the front, but I sat at the back. Most of the family didn't know about me."

"Well. They would know the baby hadn't arrived by immaculate conception," Regina said.

"No, but they were never told who the dad was, at least as far as I know, Kim never told them."

"Were you satisfied by the verdict?" Angus asked.

"No, I bloody was not. It was murder pure and simple. He should have got life that sod, but what did he get? A few years in the pokey and he can't practice as a dentist anymore. Oh, dear. What a shame for him. Damn slap on the wrist that was. They should have thrown away the key."

"Which of the witnesses did you hear?"

"I don't think there were all that many. I couldn't go on the Monday, but that first day, Kim said the jury was picked, and then a paramedic team gave evidence and a pathologist. I don't want to be a pathologist. I couldn't work with corpses all the time."

"I think we can all agree that you are not going to be a pathologist," Regina said.

"I was there the second day. It was a Tuesday. A woman detective gave evidence. My sister, as it turns out. What are the odds? She was on the dentist's side too. Bitch."

"I think you'll find she wasn't on anybody's side, she would just state what she knew."

"So you say. Anyway, I'd found her when I was researching my birth family."

"You said you stopped when you found your mother was dead," Angus reminded him.

"Yes, I did. I lied. I found them all, and where they live, what they do everything. It's not the worst thing I've done."

"What is the worst thing you've done, Troy?" Angus asked. He was taken aback when Troy stared through him as if he weren't there and laughed.

"Do you want a lawyer now, Troy?" Regina asked.

"Would it make a difference?"

"I don't know. I can't tell you that, but I can call one for you if you would like that."

He became solemn again. "I didn't know the names of the people on the jury, so I sat at the back and drew pictures of them. I'm good at drawing. It helps with anatomy classes."

"I imagine it does," Angus said.

"Then I looked on social media and found details of the trial in a gossip site. 'Dangerous Dentists' or something. It listed all the names of the jury members It wasn't difficult to find their addresses after that. I had decided, after that unforgivable verdict, I would just work my way through the jury, the witnesses, and the judge, until they had all suffered. I wanted them to die, like my wee girl."

"But you must have drawn them before the verdict," Angus said.

"Yes, I wanted to know who was making the decision. I thought I'd be able to find them and send them each a thank you note, but it wasn't like that." Troy looked at Angus. "I missed the one with the green flash in her hair. But her colleague saw me, so he had to go. I couldn't risk it. And I haven't finished yet."

"I think you'll find you have, Troy. You're completely finished now. And I will call you that lawyer."

Jallow rose from her chair and terminated the interview.

Chapter Sixty-One

DCI Mackay let Regina bring the briefing to order. The noise had been incredible. Everybody was thrilled to see Jane back at work. She stood to the side, looking particularly self-conscious and sipping a mug of chamomile tea. Angus and Amar stood beside her, probably more to be close to the large box of doughnuts she had brought in, rather than out of camaraderie. Mackay noticed that Brian and Judy were standing with a group on the other side of the room. Brian held a doughnut in each hand. Mackay deduced that any truce that had arisen between Amar and Brian during the hunt for Jane had been called off.

As the chatter subsided, Mackay began to speak, first to welcome Jane back to MIT and then to ask her to explain her decision not to push for Donny's prosecution.

"Well, sir, it's true he did stalk me, but he has since explained that he was making sure he knew my routine and where I lived so he could protect me from Troy." She smiled. "It seems like Craig and I never bothered with finding the family. Craig's a butcher, a decent bloke, by all accounts. But Donny and Troy both looked up about the family. Curiosity got the better of Troy, and Donny was asked about his birth family when he joined the military."

"But he didn't just stalk you, Jane, sorry, DS Renwick. He abducted you," Angus said as he reached for another doughnut. "You did say there's another box, didn't you?"

"Yes." She laughed. "I know, but he abducted me to keep me safe from Troy too."

"That didn't work out so well," Judy said.

"In the end, no it didn't." Jane rubbed her neck. "But that wasn't Donny's fault. Anyway, I don't want to go after him.

It'd ruin his military career."

"We will respect your wishes, even if we think you're wrong," Mackay said. "Now, DI Jallow, I believe you and DC McKenzie did a fine job with the killer."

They all listened carefully as Regina told them how Angus had teased the truth out of Troy.

"And then, it got to a point where I knew we had to get him a brief. Otherwise he might wriggle off the hook. It was a long day, wasn't it, DC McKenzie?"

"It was, boss, but it was worth keeping at it."

"He eventually admitted joining the dating agency, *Alone In A Crowd*, it's called. Dolores Cline, Beatrice Dalgleish and Lady Munro were all registered with them. He found that out by combing social media. That's how he got to them. Met them for a date and then saw them home."

"But Lady Munro was at home?" Mackay asked.

"She was. She was a bit more discreet than the other ladies and wouldn't let him see her home, but he'd found out where she lived through his searches. He said that she seemed to be expecting somebody else the night he called on her, the two of them had nothing arranged."

"And the professor? He wasn't on the books of this agency, was he?"

"Sort of, sir," Jallow said. "He had registered and attended one speed dating night, but that's not what got him killed."

"Troy was in the language department of the university because he had been watching Gillian and knew she usually had a tutorial group late on a Thursday. What he didn't know was, it had been cancelled that week. However, when he was wandering about, he went into Zelay's room by mistake and the professor challenged him. He killed Zelay because he had seen his face."

"He attacked the Edinburgh DC, Bear Zewedu, too, I understand," Mackay said.

"He said DC Zewedu just got in the way," Regina said.

"The man is mad," Brian said.

"That's probably what his legal team will argue," Mackay said. "Anyway, job well done, team. The drinks are on me tonight. In the meantime, I want the paperwork tied up as tight as a badger's bum so that maniac never injures or kills again as long as he lives." He reached for a chocolate doughnut and walked back to his office.

Chapter Sixty-Two

The doorbell rang again.

"I'll go," Rachael shouted. "Hi Bear, Mel. Come on in. Angus, Tim and Gillian are in the kitchen, I think."

"Just point me towards the food." Bear grinned. He kissed Rachael on the cheek and followed Mel into the kitchen. He saw Jane taking a large tray of sausage rolls out of the oven and putting them on a wooden board. "You've always been my favourite." He said and swiped one. He popped it in his mouth. It exited from there just as swiftly. "God, those are hot."

"You watched me take them out of the oven, Bear. What did you expect?" Jane laughed and handed Bear a can of beer.

"This is purely medicinal, you know that, right?"

"Yeh right. How you doing, big man?" Tim asked.

"Well, my arm is almost fully healed."

"But he's still not well enough to wash dishes or run the vacuum over the flat." Mel giggled. "Apparently that could take years." Two people she didn't know stood shyly in the doorway. She watched as Jane threw her arms around the man and opened the group to include the woman in the hug.

Mel nudged Angus. "Who's that?"

Angus looked up, "Jane's younger brother, Craig." He went over and shook the man firmly by the hand. "Sorry about the confusion, Craig. No hard feelings?"

"No, it's all worked out. This is Julie."

"Come and get a drink and let me introduce you."

When Amar arrived, he asked Angus. "You still okay about me staying at your place tonight?"

"Sure, as long as you don't mind the couch."

"No, I don't mind. It means I can drink. Are Brian or Judy here yet?"

"Haven't seen them."

"Good."

"This is Craig and Julie, Jane's brother and his girlfriend."

***

Tim signalled to Bear, and the two men left the group and wandered into the hall.

"What's up?" Bear asked.

"This the new phone I promised you. I bought you a year's insurance too, just in case," Tim said and handed Bear the white box.

"Tim, I can't take this, it's the brand-new iPhone. It must have cost you a fortune. My gear was an old crappy thing."

"I know, and I specifically asked in the shop for an old crappy phone, but they were right out of stock. They must be right on trend. You'll just have to make do with that."

"Thanks, Tim. That's great."

Jane walked towards them with a tall, thin man on her arm. The tattoos at the top of his chest and right up his arms were visible under his short-sleeved shirt.

"Tim, Bear, this is my brother Donny. He stalked me, scared me half to death took me captive and held me hostage, all in the name of keeping me safe. Donny, meet Tim and Bear, they were the best men when Rachael and I tied the knot."

The men shook hands.

"Just one thing, Donny. Why not just tell Jane she was in danger and help her?" Bear asked. "I mean, you didn't have to put her through all that."

"I didn't think she'd want me, or any of us back in her life. She's so amazing. I tried to ensure that she'd never know who I was and when the danger was over, I could just return her to her life without intruding on it for ever. But that didn't work so well," Donny replied. He watched Bear nod, then Donny went in search of a beer.

Tim walked behind him. "Just tell me one more thing, Donny. How did you get Jane from Dreghorn to Dundee Street without anybody noticing?"

"I stuck her in the boot of this old, bashed red car I borrowed. The guy is a regular at the pub I drink at. He said it wasn't up to much. He'd had an accident and the front was bashed, so he lent it to me for fifty quid and told me where to leave it when I'd done with it."

"We found some long hairs in the boot, I thought they might be Jane's. That's a thought, we never did get the results of that DNA back yet."

"Well, I told him I only needed it for one day, and that I'd get it back to him. He was happy enough. Said he'd get the scrap for it. I only drove it that once, to my flat in Dundee Street, and back. When I phoned to say it was back where he'd said to leave it, he told me he didn't want to keep it because he'd hit a wee girl with it, and he thought she'd died."

Everybody in the room became quiet, and Tim looked over at Craig and Julie. "Don't worry," he said. "With Donny's help, we'll get him."

Epilogue

Mackay smiled at Jallow. "How did we get on in the High Court?"

"As well as could be expected. Troy Bean was committed to Carstairs Mental Hospital for treatment. If he ever gets out, it'll be in thirty years from now."

"It's still not justice, he'll only be in his fifties."

"I know, sir, but it's as good as we were going to get."

"Yes. And the hit and run driver?"

"We got him, no problem. That Edinburgh DC, Tim Myerscough, had offered to replace his car. With his own money, I may add."

"Hmm, he's certainly got enough of it," Mackay said.

"Why's he a cop?"

"Long story. Did you know his father was a chief constable?"

"Then he must have got his money from his mother," Jallow said.

"Anyway, what has that got to do with catching the hit and run driver?"

"Myerscough arranged with the car showroom that they would have the man in at a certain time and Myerscough and Zewedu were there too with Jane's brother who could identify him. The boys arrested him."

"Did he get his car?"

"Apparently Myerscough told him he wouldn't be needing it where he was going."

Mackay chuckled. "Was he right?"

"Yes, indeed. Ten years. I believe Myerscough gave the car to the young couple whose child was killed by him instead."

"Jane's younger brother? That was good of him. Speaking

of Jane, where is she?"

"Myerscough had booked a vacation in the Seychelles for him and his girlfriend, the one who worked with Dr Zelay Scheptytsky."

"Very nice, I could do with getting away."

"Me too, sir. But the girlfriend was determined that she would accompany Zelay's body back to his homeland in the Ukraine and she has since been invited to lecture at the university in Kiev, so she couldn't go on the holiday."

"Jallow, fascinating as this all is, I just want to know where the hell DS Jane Renwick is?"

"That's what I'm trying to tell you, sir. After all they've been through, Myerscough had the names changed on the tickets and gave the trip to Jane and her partner, Rachael."

"Lucky Jane Renwick. That's just fanbloodytastic, Jallow. Why do things like that never happen to us?"

"Your guess is as good as mine, sir."

"Let me buy you lunch, Regina. We can Google the Seychelles and turn green with envy."

Jane Renwick in A Fighting Chance will follow soon.

Fantastic Books
Great Authors

darkstroke is
an imprint of
Crooked Cat Books

- Gripping Thrillers
- Cosy Mysteries
- Romantic Chick-Lit
- Fascinating Historicals
- Exciting Fantasy
- Young Adult and Children's Adventures
- Non-Fiction

Discover us online
www.darkstroke.com

Find us on instagram:
www.instagram.com/darkstrokebooks

Printed in Great Britain
by Amazon